THE CAPTAIN AND THE DUCHESS

The Strongs of Shadowcrest
Book Four

Alexa Aston

➤➤➤◄◄◄

Dearest Reader;

Thank you for your support of a small press. At Dragonblade Publishing, we strive to bring you the highest quality Historical Romance from some of the best authors in the business. Without your support, there is no 'us', so we sincerely hope you adore these stories and find some new favorite authors along the way.

Happy Reading!

CEO, Dragonblade Publishing

Additional Dragonblade books by Author Alexa Aston

The Strongs of Shadowcrest Series
The Duke's Unexpected Love (Book 1)
The Perks of Loving a Viscount (Book 2)
Falling for the Marquess (Book 3)
The Captain and the Duchess (Book 4)

Suddenly a Duke Series
Portrait of the Duke (Book 1)
Music for the Duke (Book 2)
Polishing the Duke (Book 3)
Designs on the Duke (Book 4)
Fashioning the Duke (Book 5)
Love Blooms with the Duke (Book 6)
Training the Duke (Book 7)
Investigating the Duke (Book 8)

Second Sons of London Series
Educated By The Earl (Book 1)
Debating With The Duke (Book 2)
Empowered By The Earl (Book 3)
Made for the Marquess (Book 4)
Dubious about the Duke (Book 5)
Valued by the Viscount (Book 6)
Meant for the Marquess (Book 7)

Dukes Done Wrong Series
Discouraging the Duke (Book 1)
Deflecting the Duke (Book 2)
Disrupting the Duke (Book 3)

Destined for Love (Book 3)

Knights of Honor Series
Word of Honor (Book 1)
Marked by Honor (Book 2)
Code of Honor (Book 3)
Journey to Honor (Book 4)
Heart of Honor (Book 5)
Bold in Honor (Book 6)
Love and Honor (Book 7)
Gift of Honor (Book 8)
Path to Honor (Book 9)
Return to Honor (Book 10)

The Lyon's Den Series
The Lyon's Lady Love

Pirates of Britannia Series
God of the Seas

De Wolfe Pack: The Series
Rise of de Wolfe

The de Wolfes of Esterley Castle
Diana
Derek
Thea

Also from Alexa Aston
The Bridge to Love (Novella)
One Magic Night

PROLOGUE

Shadowcrest—October 1809

D INAH STRONG, WIDOWED Duchess of Seaton, looked around the table as her girls chatted happily during breakfast.

It was good to be back at Shadowcrest.

She, her daughters, and nieces had all been forced to remain in London the past three years while her husband lay dying. The Duke of Seaton, twenty-five years her senior, had suffered an attack of apoplexy. It had left him bedridden, unable to communicate, lingering between life and death.

Dinah would have brought him home to the country and tended to him at Shadowcrest, but her brother-in-law, Adolphus Strong, had forbid her from taking the duke to his country estate in Kent. Instead, the duke's twin assumed his brother's ducal power and all but title, assuming he would become the next Duke of Seaton following his brother's death. Adolphus had kept the women housebound, isolating them from all others in Polite Society, and they had lived in a gloomy state while Adolphus and his older son Theodore gadded about town, spending money that wasn't theirs.

All that had recently changed, thanks to the return of her stepson James. James was the son of Seaton's first wife, who had died in childbirth after delivering a stillborn son. The duke wed Dinah when she was only ten and seven, expecting her to give him numerous sons, especially after James disappeared on the London docks when he was only eight years of age, never to be seen again.

Instead, Dinah had birthed four daughters. Her husband had called her worthless. He had finally stopped coming to her bed when he could no longer perform his marital duties.

She had been only one and twenty years old.

She had still done everything she could to be the best wife she could be. Known as an excellent hostess, she planned lavish social events. While she received no affection from her husband, she had come to live for her daughters and the two nieces she had raised. Adolphus had no interest in females. When his own wife perished after giving birth to Lyric and Allegra, her brother-in-law had dumped the twins upon her to bring up.

Dinah had not minded. She had more than enough love in her heart for those two motherless girls and considered them her own. She had raised them alongside her own twins Georgina and Pippa, and added Mirella and Effie to the nursery shortly afterward.

With James returning to England, the former sea captain had ousted Adolphus and Theodore from the household. James had assumed the dukedom when his father passed, allowing Dinah and her girls to return to their beloved Shadowcrest for the first time in more than three years. Breathing the country air once more and having the freedom to roam the estate had done all of them good. It had also been nice to reunite with Aunt Matty, her husband's sister, who had been exiled by Adolphus to Shadowcrest for daring to stand up to him and question him taking on the duke's authority while he still lived.

"What are your plans today, my darlings?" Dinah asked.

Pippa spoke up first, as she usually did. "Effie and I are going to ride. Miss Feathers said Effie does not have to report for her lessons until one o'clock. We plan to be gone until then."

Both Pippa and Effie were tomboys and enjoyed being in the saddle or hunting and fishing. She knew how difficult it had been on both of them, having to remain inside the townhouse during those three years with no walks in Hyde Park nor rides in Rotten Row.

"That sounds lovely," she said. "What about the rest of you?"

"Lyric and I are going to be working in the gardens," Allegra volunteered.

Lyric explained what they would be doing, her eyes lighting with enthusiasm as they always did when she talked about her beloved flowers. Her nieces were quite close, being twins, and she was glad to see Allegra taking an interest in gardening. Usually, that was what Lyric spent most of her time doing.

"Well, it is a lovely day. I am certain you will enjoy spending it outdoors." She turned to her other two daughters. "And what might the two of you be up to?"

"Mirella and I are going to do our usual pianoforte practice, Mama," Georgina said. "Then we are going to walk into the village and meet with the clergyman's wife. She is interested in forming a children's choir and thinks Mirella and I could help her in this endeavor."

Those two daughters were the most musically inclined in the Strong family, and Dinah had encouraged them in their playing. She knew music had saved Georgina and Mirella during the long years of being forced to remain inside.

"That sounds wonderful," she declared. "And Aunt Matty? What are you up to today?"

"I am visiting with Lady Chatham this morning. I will be on my way to see her soon. But what of you, Dinah?"

"I plan to take a long walk and then read in the garden. This may be one of the last warm days we have, so I want to soak up the sunshine while I can."

Soon, everyone had gone their separate ways, and Dinah leisurely walked through the meadow at Shadowcrest. She reveled in her newfound freedom, not only being out from under Adolphus' thumb, but also having no husband for the first time in almost two decades. Of course, her first obligation was to her six girls. Next spring, Georgina and Pippa would make their come-outs, along with Allegra and Lyric. Mirella would follow the next year, and Effie would two years after that.

But Dinah was now free from her unwanted marriage. She toyed with the idea of possibly taking a lover—or even a husband. She was in her mid-thirties and still had her looks.

What would it be like if she could actually find love?

She had fancied herself in love many years ago. A local baron had a handsome son two years her senior. He had asked her to dance at the local assemblies and sat next to her at church. They had talked of books, and she had played the pianoforte for him, with him singing along off-key. Dinah had wanted to marry him, especially after he sweetly kissed her. She wanted to have babies with him and live a quiet life in the country, the thought of being a part of the *ton* not appealing to her.

Of course, her parents had other plans. Her father, in particular, was conscious of titles. He told Dinah her beauty would draw in the wealthiest of men in Polite Society, with titles she could only dream of holding. She hadn't cared one whit about being a duchess or marchioness, but she was told she could never marry the boy who held her heart. Instead, arrangements were made without her knowing, and she was betrothed to the much-older Duke of Seaton, a widower in his forties, who had one son and was looking for more.

After having been a dutiful daughter and wife all these years, Dinah decided it was time she would live for herself. While her priority was to see that her daughters made good matches, she would never force them to wed strictly for a title. She hoped her girls would find love.

And that she might, as well.

Perhaps when the two sets of twins made their come-outs next spring, Dinah herself would leave the section where the matrons sat and actually dance with a few partners herself. The thought grew on her, and she decided to think more on it in the months to come. She might find a widower amongst the *ton* who looked for another wife, or even a gentleman who had never wed. She only knew she had been pushed into one marriage, and that would never occur again. If she ever did wed a second time, it would be strictly for love, that all-too-fragile feeling. And if no man stirred such feelings within her, then she would enjoy her life as a widow. Widows in Polite Society had more freedom than wives. She would pursue her interests and take an active role as a grandmother. With six girls, numerous grandchildren would certainly make their debuts.

Dinah returned from her long walk and chose a book from the library, bringing it outside and taking a seat on the terrace because the sun was so plentiful there. For October, it was unseasonably warm. The weather could quickly change this time of year, though, and she was determined to enjoy being outdoors for as long as she could, now that she had the freedom to be outside as she pleased.

She had only read a few pages when Forrester appeared, looking distressed.

"Your Grace, there is a man here demanding to see you."

Frowning, she asked, "What man? What is his name?"

"He looks most unsuitable, Your Grace. I have tried to get him to leave, but he insists upon seeing you immediately."

"Where is he—"

"Your Grace?" A voice from inside the house roared. "Your Grace? I must see Her Grace at once!"

She recognized the voice. A tingle shot through her.

"Is it Captain Andrews?"

The butler looked stunned. "Yes, that was the name he gave."

"Bring him here at once, Forrester."

The butler didn't have to do so because Drake Andrews bounded through the open French door, glancing about, looking for her.

Then their gazes met—and her heart skipped a beat.

The handsome sea captain was covered in soot, his face and hands blackened. His clothing was disheveled and they, too, were covered in soot. As he drew close, he smelled like smoke, so much that her eyes began to water.

"Whatever has happened to you, Captain Andrews?" Dinah asked, her pulse pounding as she looked at his lean, athletic frame and handsome face.

"It is His Grace," Andrews said, looking as if he were about to collapse.

"Have a seat, Captain," she insisted, taking his elbow and guiding him to a chair. Looking to Forrester, she said, "Bring hot tea at once. And heat water for a bath."

"There's no time for that," the sea captain spat out.

She looked at him steadily. "Whatever it is, Captain, you look to be half-dead. A cup of tea and a bath will revive you. Once you have had both, we can address the problem." Glancing to the butler again, she said, "At once, Forrester. And find Captain Andrews some suitable clothes. Something from His Grace's closet might fit."

Her husband had been perhaps an inch taller or so, but she believed something of the duke's would fit this man.

As Forrester scurried away, Dinah sat. "Gather your thoughts, Captain," she said gently. "Then tell me everything. Leave nothing out. Take your time."

Drake Andrews let out a long sigh. He closed his eyes, composing himself, then opened them again.

"James—His Grace—helped fight a fire last night. It broke out at the Strong Shipping warehouse. He was on the front lines of the fire brigade and inhaled much of the smoke."

Panic filled her, but she remained calm outwardly. "Is he alive?"

"Yes. Under a doctor's care. But he needs a woman's touch, Your Grace. I thought it best for his family to help care for him until he is on his feet again. I would stay, but I am to leave soon, sailing *Vesta* to the South Seas."

She placed her hand over his filthy one. "I know you have been like a brother to James all these years. I appreciate your thoughtfulness in bringing me this news. I hope you left your mount in our stables to be cared for."

He laughed aloud. "I do not ride, Your Grace. I've been at sea my entire life. Before that, I was living on the streets, an orphan who stole food to survive. No, I took the mail coach down to fetch you and walked from the village to Shadowcrest after I was dropped there."

Despite his mean background, Dinah felt a pull toward this man. She had the first time James had introduced them, as well, teaching Drake Andrews how to bow to a duke and how to kiss a lady's hand upon being introduced. They had flirted a bit, but she had thought never to see him again. Now he was here, doing strange things to her insides.

"We will take one of the ducal carriages back to town," she told him. "It will be much faster than a mail coach, Captain."

He frowned. "Wouldn't that be against the rules, Your Grace? You riding in a carriage with me the entire way to London? James has told me the *ton* has all kinds of things to say about the behavior of its members, particularly female ones."

She bit back a smile. "That is kind of you to be concerned for my reputation, Captain Andrews, but a widow has a bit more freedom than a young miss or wife in Polite Society. You will serve as my escort back to town, but you will need to clean up in order to do so. James will be resting in bed for the next several days. An hour will not make that much difference."

The tea cart arrived, and she poured him a cup of tea, doctoring it so it was quite sweet and strong.

Handing it over, she said, "Drink this. I will have my maid go and pack a few things for me. I will stay a week or so, at least until James is on his feet again. By the time you finish your cup of tea, your bath should be prepared. Once you have bathed and dressed, we shall depart for town at once."

He looked at her gratefully. "I appreciate you coming to attend to James, Your Grace. He is all the family I have." Smiling ruefully, he added, "Even if he is a duke now and should have nothing to do with the likes of me."

"Do not say such things," she chided. "You are a loyal friend of many years. James would not cast aside his friendship with you simply because he is now a duke. If anything, he would choose you above anyone else."

He placed his hand atop hers, causing a ripple of warmth to flood her. "You are right, Your Grace. About everything. I will drink my tea and clean up and escort you to London and James' side."

"Town," she prompted, smiling at him. "We call it town. Never London."

The corners of his mouth turned up. "Another lesson you're teaching me, Your Grace?"

She shrugged. "You never know when those lessons might come in handy, Captain."

Dinah stepped away, reluctantly breaking the contact between them. She had the strongest urge to kiss this handsome sailor. She had not kissed anyone in almost twenty years. She and her sweetheart had traded a few chaste kisses before her marriage to Seaton. The duke had never kissed her. Not once.

But more than anything, Dinah desired to kiss Drake Andrews. If any man could show her what kissing was about, it was the flirtatious, handsome seaman.

An hour later, her things were packed and the trunk secured to the ducal carriage. She was leaving her maid behind, telling the girl that

Mrs. Powell, the duke's housekeeper in town, could help her in dressing. Though all the girls had demanded to go to town with her, she knew a bevy of women was the last thing James needed about him as he convalesced.

A footman handed her into the carriage, and Captain Andrews climbed in after her, sitting beside her. She found her side pressed against his, liking the warmth.

"You no longer smell like smoke," she said playfully. "That will make for a more pleasant journey to town."

He laughed, showing white, even teeth. His deep brown eyes gleamed at her as he said, "And look at the finery I now wear. I was told by the butler that these clothes belonged to your late husband."

"Well, he no longer has need of them," she said lightly. "I am glad they were of use to you."

"Your housekeeper refused to give my clothes back to me," he informed her. "Said the soot would never come out of them. She told me she had burned them."

"Oh! I am so sorry, Captain Andrews. I will have them replaced."

"It's quite all right, Your Grace. They were civilian clothes. I will be wearing my new captain's uniform soon."

"Are you more confident in your position now?" she asked, recalling how he had expressed the opinion that he did not have the experience required to take on command of a sailing vessel.

His gaze pinned hers. "You did not even know me—yet you told me to believe in myself. I took your advice, Your Grace. I accepted Mrs. Grant's offer to captain *Vesta*, and I am confident in my abilities to lead my crew during this upcoming voyage." He chuckled. "I will simply imitate James every step of the way. The new duke is a leader among men, no matter what part of society they fall into."

They enjoyed a pleasant conversation over the next couple of hours, with Captain Andrews telling her about many of the ports he had seen over his seafaring years.

"Do you ever wish to remain on land?" she asked. "Stay in one place? Raise a family?"

A faraway look appeared in his eyes. "I never thought to have a family. Seamen are gone so often from home. I thought that would be unfair to a woman, being away for long stretches at a time. Would I like a family, though, beyond my fellow sailors? I believe I would.

"As for remaining in once place? I have no idea how I would earn my living or what I would do."

She smiled. "Perhaps you might learn to ride a horse, Captain."

He laughed heartily. "Actually, I would like that. I like animals, cats, in particular. We keep a few on board, to keep the rats at bay. But it's only fine gentlemen who ride horses, not the likes of me, Your Grace."

Dinah thought him a gentleman in behavior, if not one by birth, but she also understood he would never be accepted by society because of his humble origins. It was a pity—because she thought the sinfully handsome sea captain would be a man who could show her much about bed sport.

They arrived at the ducal townhouse, and Captain Andrews saw her safely inside. They went to the duke's rooms and found the doctor with James. He informed Dinah of the duke's condition, informing her that His Grace was still confused and had some difficulty breathing, but he was past the worse of things.

"I will come again tomorrow to check on His Grace, but I will leave him in your hands for now, Your Grace."

"Thank you, Doctor," she said. "I am grateful for all you have done for His Grace."

After the physician left, Captain Andrews said, "I must also say farewell, Your Grace. I need to return to *Vesta*."

"I will certainly let James know you were here and that you brought me to town to care for him." She took his hand and squeezed it. "You are a good friend to him, Captain. I hope you won't be a stranger to us all in the future. Please, come and see us once you return from your voyage."

"That will be next July or August, Your Grace," he told her. "But I would appreciate coming to see you and having a cup of tea."

"Then plan on it, Captain."

"I will see myself out," he said.

Dinah watched him leave, feeling the sea captain left with a small piece of her heart.

CHAPTER ONE

London—July 1810

C APTAIN DRAKE ANDREWS left *Vesta*, moving swiftly down the gangplank and across the London docks. His first mate was overseeing the unloading of cargo which had been brought back from half a world away. The manager of the Neptune Shipping Lines' warehouse was also on hand, supervising his workers as sailors brought up goods and crates, and the workers loaded them into wagons. As he walked toward the Neptune Shipping offices, he saw the steady stream of wagons passing him, destined for the warehouse, where they would be sorted and hauled to various sections.

It was good to finally be in London again. No, town. Drake couldn't help but smile at the distinction, taught to him by the Duchess of Seaton. The woman had stayed with him over the past several months he was at sea. Drake thought it was wrong to even think of the unattainable beauty. She was so far above his station, it would be impossible to do the things he wanted to do to her.

But had he certainly thought of those many things during his long nights at sea.

He was as common as they came. Didn't even recall his given name. He'd lived on the streets after both his parents died, digging through the rubbish for old crusts of bread, stealing food when he could. At some point, he found himself near the London Docks, and a grizzled sailor named Flimm had snatched him up. Drake had been too small to fight back, and the sailor had taken him aboard a vessel which sailed the next day. He'd found himself being called Boy for a couple of years as he served as a cabin boy.

Once he finally earned the right to his name, he had no idea what it was. He had been Boy for so long. Instead, he had chosen a name—Drake—which was a male duck who took to water. His surname of Andrews came from a captain he admired. And thus, Drake Andrews had come into existence.

Working his way up, he had finally been made First Mate to his closest friend, James, another supposed orphan such as himself. They had grown up together, thick as thieves, Drake being a dozen years older and watching over the small boy who grew to be quite a large man. When James learned of his true identity, he'd stepped away from a life at sea. Mrs. Grant, who ran Neptune Shipping Lines after the death of her husband, had taken James' advice and made Drake the new captain of *Vesta*. It would be Mrs. Grant whom he reported to today.

Or perhaps not. His gut told him the feelings James had displayed for the pretty widow might have resulted in a marriage between the pair during Drake's absence. If so, Neptune Shipping Lines now belonged to his friend, the new Duke of Seaton, as did Strong Shipping, the family business. He wondered if James would merge the two lines. Why, he might be headed to an office which no longer existed.

The Neptune Shipping offices came into sight, however, and he supposed he might have gotten things wrong. He would soon learn after giving his report to Mrs. Grant—or whoever was running the shipping empire now.

Inside the offices, he saw Mr. Samuel, who informed Drake he was now the company's secretary.

"And what of Mr. Barnes?" he inquired, referring to the previous secretary, a man who had served as Mrs. Grant's right-hand man.

"I will inform Mr. Barnes you are here," Mr. Samuel said.

So, Mr. Barnes now ran Neptune. That meant his guess of James wedding and bedding Mrs. Grant must have come to pass. Once he spoke with Mr. Barnes, Drake would next visit his old friend.

Mr. Samuel excused himself and was gone a few minutes. When he returned, he informed Drake he could see Mr. Barnes now.

The former secretary greeted him. "Welcome back to England, Captain Andrews. I was informed *Vesta* had arrived. I hope all went well?"

"Better than expected, Mr. Barnes. We were able to bring back a third more of whale oil than anticipated. Also, we have excess Merino wool."

Barnes smiled broadly. "That is excellent news, Captain. If you will hand over your log, I will review it with Her Grace. Let us sit and discuss the particulars now."

"I assume Mrs. Grant is now Her Grace?" Drake asked, passing his log book to the man and taking the seat Barnes indicated.

"Oh, yes, that occurred soon after you left port. The Duke of Seaton wed Mrs. Grant in October."

"And you are now running Neptune for His Grace?"

Barnes laughed heartily. "Not at all. Your friend said his family had its own shipping line, and he had no need of his wife's. In a most unusual move—which shocked Polite Society—His Grace allowed Her Grace to keep Neptune Shipping Lines as her own. The duchess still runs it, Captain Andrews. I merely aid her in doing so."

He grinned. It was just like James to do something such as this.

"While Strong Shipping will go to the ducal heir, any other children from the marriage will share in Neptune Shipping and run it someday." Now, Mr. Barnes was the one smiling. "Her Grace is with child even now, the babe due near the end of September. She and His

Grace have retired to Kent to await the birth of the babe. I go down every week or so to keep Her Grace apprised of business affairs. Let me tell you, Captain, the duchess continues to run Neptune, and she is teaching His Grace quite a bit about business."

If anyone could catch on to business, it would be his friend. James was the most intelligent man of Drake's acquaintance.

"I am happy to hear all of this, Mr. Barnes."

They got down to business after that, with Drake giving a detailed account of the voyage *Vesta* had been on. Only slight damage had occurred to the vessel while at sea, during a lightning storm, but he shared that repairs had been made and that new ones shouldn't take long. Trade had been profitable, and all the goods the ship had left with were exchanged. After two hours, they had completed their discussion.

"I will write up everything we have discussed from the notes I have taken and present them to Her Grace." Barnes paused. "Unless you will be traveling to Shadowcrest to visit with Their Graces."

"It depends upon how soon I will be sent back to sea, Mr. Barnes, though I would like to see them."

"You brought *Vesta* back in record time, Captain Andrews. We were not expecting you until late July at the earliest and most likely mid-August. Because of that, you are not scheduled to return to sea until at least September. Most likely, you would set sail the second week of that month."

It would give him the longest he had ever spent in London.

And Drake had a good idea where he would head next.

"Then I would be happy to present your report to Her Grace in person," he offered.

"Give me a few days then, Captain. I will also include in it the exact figures I receive from the warehouse and the goods which have been brought back by you to England." Barnes thought a moment. "I am scheduled to visit with Her Grace in about a week's time. Come back next Tuesday, a week from today, and I will give you my report to take with you."

"I am glad I can save you a trip, Mr. Barnes. I will see you Tuesday next."

That would give him a week in town. A week to visit the now Dowager Duchess of Seaton.

And a week to make his fantasies become a reality.

Drake left the Neptune Shipping offices, walking a few blocks away from the docks in order to find a hansom cab. He gave the coachman the address for the Duke of Seaton's townhouse. He had first accompanied James to the grand house when his friend thought he might be related to the Strongs. That visit had been a little less than a year ago. Now, with the old duke's death, James had inherited the London townhouse, Shadowcrest in Kent, and several properties scattered throughout England, not to mention owning Strong Shipping, one of the world's largest shipping empires. To think the lost little boy he had met years ago, beaten to within an inch of his life, had become one of the most powerful men in Great Britain still boggled Drake's mind.

But he had other things on his mind now. First and foremost, he wanted to see James' stepmother. It was hard to think of the beautiful duchess in that way. She had only been a decade older than her stepson when she wed the Duke of Seaton. James was now six and twenty, which put the duchess in her mid-thirties. At two years shy of forty, he and the widow were quite close in age.

The question was if she would be willing to spend the kind of intimate time with him that he wished. He had always been a ladies' man, acknowledging his good looks and ready smile, both always getting him what he wanted from women in ports around the world.

But what Drake wanted now was to couple with a woman far too good for him. It wasn't hard to bring up the topic with women he met in taverns around the world. Half the time, *they* were the ones who flirted outrageously with him, letting him know just how willing they were to have him in their beds.

He had done his best to try and forget the duchess over the last several months. He had made love to a good dozen women, women of all ages and looks, and yet each encounter left him deeply unsatisfied. He had lain sleeplessly in his bunk aboard *Vesta*, the image of one woman burned into his memory.

Drake decided the old adage *nothing ventured, nothing gained* applied in these circumstances. It was a risk approaching a woman of her rank in society, asking her to couple with him. He wasn't expecting a successful outcome. But if things did turn out in his favor, Drake thought it would be the most incredibly satisfying experience of his life.

And hopefully, hers.

The hansom cab entered the square where James' townhouse was located. He paid the cabby and approached the door, nerves skirting through him. With determination, he raised his hand and rapped on the door.

⫸⫷

DINAH SAID FAREWELL to her last suitor, relieved that no visitors would be staying for tea.

She had truly tried this Season to be open to finding love within the *ton*. Sadly, it had not happened for her. Thank goodness it had for Georgina, her only daughter making her come-out this Season. Georgina had wed the Marquess of Edgethorne a little over a month ago, and they had traveled first to Edgefield for Georgina to see her new home in the country. Then August had taken them to Dalmara, a property he had inherited from his mother in Scotland. The pair were currently honeymooning there and would most likely be back in mid-September. Dinah had high hopes that Georgina would be with child when she returned.

Pippa had also wed for love, marrying their neighbor in Kent, Lord Hopewell, a former sea captain. Her daughter and husband were also honeymooning, except their journey was taking them around the globe. Pippa had always had a desire to see far-off lands, and Seth was only too happy to be his new wife's escort. They would be gone a good eighteen months and possibly longer. It would be lovely if Pippa and Seth arrived home with a child. Dinah would be so pleased to be a grandmother twice over.

She took a seat in the drawing room, knowing the teacart would be arriving soon. James and Sophie had returned to Shadowcrest after they hosted a ball in Georgina's honor, where her betrothal to Edgethorne was announced. After the wedding, the Duke and Duchess of Seaton remained in the country, where Sophie would give birth to their firstborn near the end of September.

Dinah had returned to town, hoping that now her twin daughters were happily wed, she herself might find a gentleman which suited her. Alas, they all seemed the same to her. Boring. Ignorant of current affairs. Even men her age and older who had never wed before still acted as boys instead of men. While she had been slightly interested in two or three gentlemen, one a widower with two young boys, she had not felt that spark which she was looking for.

The one she had only felt with a man wholly unsuitable to be her husband.

Captain Drake Andrews.

The handsome sea captain had remained in her thoughts ever since he had brought her to town to care for James after the warehouse fire. Andrews had left almost immediately for a voyage, the first in which he would captain a ship of his own, the very one James had once been in charge of. Dinah recalled that carriage ride from Shadowcrest to town. How they had talked about a variety of topics. How interesting the captain was.

And how attractive he was.

She was a widow, a woman who had latitude in Polite Society. Many widows had discreet affairs throughout the Season, but those were with other gentlemen of the *ton*, not men who worked to earn their living. Yet Dinah could not think of a single man who had intrigued her the way Drake Andrews did. It was wrong, but she had thought of him almost every night since they had parted. She would lie in bed, waiting for sleep to come, and her mind was filled with images of him. Flirting. Laughing. Smiling at her.

If the man returned to England before the Season ended, surely he would call upon them, wouldn't he? After all, James was his greatest friend and the brother of his heart. If Captain Andrews did come to visit, how on earth would she go about asking him if he wished to have a brief affair with her? What did one say to a prospective paramour? How did that even come up in conversation?

"I am being ridiculous," she told herself aloud. "I may never see the man again and if I did, I certainly could never bring myself to voice such notions to him. Resign yourself, Dinah, to the fact you may never find love. See to your girls—and Caleb. Help them to find happiness. It is enough to be free of a marriage you never wanted."

Her words comforted her. She would never again have to lie in a bed, motionless, waiting for a husband to perform his marital duties. She would not have to do anything or go anywhere she did not wish to go. She was a captain in her own right, sailing along in life as she now chose to do.

She also had Crestridge, the estate given to her in Seaton's will. It consisted of a decent-sized manor house and several acres. It lay about ten miles from Shadowcrest, just the other side of Crestview, the local village. It was time she gave consideration to moving to it with Mirella, Effie, and her nieces. James and Sophie were now the Duke and Duchess of Seaton. Shadowcrest was theirs. While they would never chase her away, she knew they would be growing their own family and creating memories at the country estate.

First, though, she would hold the house party she had promised Allegra and Lyric. Her nieces had chosen not to make their come-outs with Georgina this spring, upset that their father had used up their dowries and would not contribute a farthing to their expensive come-out wardrobes. Worse, Adolphus and Theodore had tried to kidnap Sophie and hold her for ransom. James had seen the pair received justice, sending them to Australia on one of his ships without a penny to their names, with instructions to drop them off and prevent them from reboarding. Dinah hoped they would remain half a world away.

In the meantime, she had convinced her nieces to allow her to at least host a house party in their honor at the end of August. It would give Lyric and Allegra the chance to meet some charming gentlemen in a more intimate setting. Dinah had high hopes that the girls would find a suitable match. Even now, she was watching the gentlemen of the *ton* carefully, seeing which seemed to be honest, affable men, ones who would make for appropriate husbands for the girls she considered her own.

A light tap sounded. Powell entered the drawing room, followed by a maid rolling in the teacart.

"Yes, Powell?" she asked, wondering why the butler was here.

"You have another caller, Your Grace."

"Oh, bother. Not another one," she complained. "I had anticipated a quiet teatime alone. Who could possibly want to interrupt it?"

"Captain Andrews, Your Grace. He arrived today and was calling on His Grace and Her Grace. When I informed him they were at Shadowcrest, he asked to see you."

She felt heat flood her cheeks. "Then please show him in, Powell. And have another teacup sent up if you would."

"Yes, Your Grace."

The butler and maid left the drawing room. Dinah took three slow, deep breaths before the butler returned, announcing, "Captain

Andrews, Your Grace."

She rose as he entered the room, looking tall, his face tanned from his days on the open waters. He came toward her, stopping, and bowed just as she had taught him to do.

"Your Grace," he said in a low rumble, his dark brown eyes gleaming as he accepted her offered hand and kissed her bare fingers.

A ripple raced through her. Anticipation? Desire?

It didn't matter. He was here. Now.

And she wanted him.

Still holding her hand, he said, "It is good to see you again, Your Grace. You look well."

"You do, as well, Captain Andrews."

She pulled on her hand gently, thinking he would release it.

He didn't.

"Captain?" she asked, her brows arching.

He kissed her fingers again. "You do not know how I have longed to do that very thing," he told her, his voice low and rough.

Dinah swallowed—and then committed to a course of action which might change her life.

"You do not know how I have yearned for you to do that—and more, Captain. Much, much more."

CHAPTER TWO

*H*AD HE HEARD *her right?*

Drake gazed into eyes of azure blue, emotions running through him which he had never felt before. They should frighten him.

But they didn't.

Instead, he said, "What do you want of me, Duchess?"

She bit her bottom lip in hesitation, causing a surge of desire to swell within him. Something told him this woman had no idea how much she appealed to him.

"Go ahead. Tell me your darkest desires," he encouraged.

Her eyes widened in surprise, but his words caused her to smile.

"I have been thinking about you, Captain. Much more than I should have. I will admit that you made quite an impression on me at our first meeting."

He returned her smile. "I remember flirting outrageously with you. How I couldn't seem to help myself."

"You are a very attractive man, Captain Andrews. At that first meeting, I was responding to your appearance alone. But the second time we met—when you came and escorted me to town—I saw you were more than your good looks. You displayed loyalty and integrity. You have been a steadfast friend—no, brother—to James. I may be his stepmama, but he is now a good friend to me, as well."

Holding her gaze, Drake asked, "And do you wish for us to be . . . good friends? Or more?"

They gazed at one another wordlessly, the tension between them palpable. Until a knock sounded at the drawing room door.

Immediately, she sprang away from him and dropped into a seat. For his part, Drake placed his hands behind his back, linking his fingers together, as a maid entered the room. She bore a teacup and saucer, bringing them across the room, and setting them on the tea tray.

"Do you need Cook to prepare any more sandwiches since you have a guest, Your Grace?"

Drake marveled at how composed the duchess was, sitting placidly, as if she hadn't a care in the world.

"No, thank you. I am not very hungry myself. Captain Andrews will be more than satisfied with what is on the tea tray."

The maid bobbed a curtsey, leaving the room and closing the door behind her.

The duchess had not moved, so he took a seat beside her on the settee. She reached for the teapot and poured out for them both, adding sugar and milk to each cup before handing his saucer to him. Drake took it, just to have something to do with his hands. To keep them off her.

For now.

He took a sip of the hot tea, knowing it soothed him.

"Shall I make up a plate for you?" she asked, playing the perfect hostess. "You must be hungry after your time at sea, eating the same things, over and over. I know as a captain you are fed better than the rest of the crew. At least that is what James has shared. But I suppose it must be nice to be on land, sitting in a drawing room, taking tea without having to worry about running an entire ship."

"It is nice because I sit here with you," he said huskily.

She raised her own teacup, and he saw her hand tremble slightly, knowing he affected her as much as she did him.

"Please eat," she told him. "I am not hungry, as I mentioned, and we would not want to hurt Cook's feelings."

He arched a brow at her. "You are concerned about your cook's feelings?"

"Of course, I am. Cook is a valued member of this household. I always want our servants to be happy in their work and to know their efforts are appreciated. Are you hungry or not?"

He set down the saucer, facing her. "I am hungry. For *you*, Duchess."

She shivered in response, and Drake covered one of her hands with his, thinking how dainty and fragile she was. He liked everything about her, from her honey-colored hair to her petite height. And he longed to touch those round, plump breasts. To caress them. To tongue them.

"You really should address me as Your Grace, Captain," she told him, and he worried she was trying to put distance between them, when all he wanted to do was close the social gap between them. Or simply ignore it.

"What do you want of me?" he asked again. "You said I have been in your thoughts all these many months. I will tell you that it has been the same for me."

A pleased look appeared upon her face. "Truly? I would have assumed you would not have given me a second thought. That you are one of those men who find a willing woman in every port you call upon, and that I would long be forgotten by you."

He threaded their fingers together. "It is true that I am no stranger to women. I like them quite a bit. And yes, every time I go ashore, I find a new one to pass the time with." Drake swallowed, deciding to be completely honest with her. "I kept to my usual pattern on this latest voyage, but it did me no good."

"How so?" she asked, concern written across her delicate brow.

"Every time I coupled with a woman, I was left unsatisfied. Empty.

Alone. Because she simply wasn't you."

She drew in a quick breath, her cheeks pinkening, surprise in her eyes. "You truly thought of me?"

"I have done nothing *but* think of you. There are many days at sea when the vastness of the ocean seems to swallow you up. I thought of you during those times. Times when I stood on the deck at night, gazing up at the stars, wondering what you were doing half a world away."

Tears misted in her eyes. "Your words move me greatly, Captain, but I do not know if they are truthful ones or not. Because I do not know you well enough."

"Don't you, Duchess?" he asked roughly, his free hand taking her chin in hand when she tried to turn away from him.

"I want to know you," she admitted. "All of you," she added, her voice a whisper.

Desire rippled through him, hearing her voice that. Yet doubt lingered. This woman had everything. What would she want with him?

"Why?" he asked.

"I have lived a very sheltered life," she explained. "I believed I was in love many years ago before I even made my come-out. I traded a few, sweet kisses with a neighbor's son, and I fancied a life with him. His father was only a baron, however. That was not good enough for my father. He wanted to improve his own standing amongst the *ton*, and that meant using the tools he had at hand."

"You," Drake guessed.

"Yes. He arranged a marriage for me with a man who held an impressive title and a vast amount of wealth."

"Your duke."

She nodded. "The Duke of Seaton. He was in his forties and a widower with a son, a man looking for a young wife to give him many more sons. Do you know he never even kissed me? He came to my bed only a handful of times during those early years. I gave birth to Georgina and Pippa less than a year after our wedding. I was barely eight and ten at that time."

The duchess sighed. "Mirella followed the next year, and Effie two years after that. Seaton only touched me twice after Effie's birth. Both times, he could not perform the marital act when he did so. He blamed me for it, saying he would never return to my bed again. I felt nothing but relief."

She looked at him longingly. "Do you know how many years that has been? I have never known love. I have never felt the loving touch of a man's hands on my body. I have lived for my girls all these years. Now, I am ready to live for myself."

Drake cradled her cheek with his palm. "Thank you for your honesty. I will tell you that I have never known love myself. I have doubted its very existence. I do have experience and know how to make a woman come alive. I cannot offer you love since I do not understand it, but I am more than willing to couple with you. To teach you the ways of intimacy. If you are willing to take that leap of faith with me, that is."

"Yes," she whispered, in a voice like a caress. "I want to see what I have missed out on all these years. The physical aspects of lovemaking. At my age, I doubt I will ever find love as Pippa and Georgina have, but I feel I owe it to myself to explore my sensual nature. If you are willing to teach me about it, Captain, I would be most grateful."

Strong emotions welled within him, ones he had never experienced in the company of another woman. It couldn't be love. That was not possible. She was a duchess, and he but a common sailor. Still, he held more desire for this woman than he had any other.

"I am hungry for you, Duchess. That is desire. I want to devour you—but I will take things slowly with you. Guide you into the pleasures of the flesh. The first thing you need to do is to learn how to kiss. If you only traded a few, chaste kisses with your sweetheart many years ago, you truly have no idea how powerful a kiss can be."

"Think of me as a block of soft clay in your hands, Captain. Un-formed. Teach me what I should know. Open a new world for me. Mold me with your hands."

He smiled down at her. "With pleasure."

Drake brought up his other hand, framing her face with his long fingers. He dipped his head to hers, pressing his lips softly against hers. They were plump, and he longed to bite into them. He held back, though, knowing he must take things slowly. He would enjoy going on this journey with her. Where it might lead, he didn't know. He simply knew he wanted to take it with her—and her alone.

Slowly, he brushed his lips against hers, back and forth, getting to know the feel and shape of them. She placed her palms against his chest, and he reveled in the warmth that simple gesture on her part brought to him.

He began kissing her, mixing soft kisses with slightly harder ones. He slipped one hand about her nape, the other around her waist, anchoring her. Inhaling her scent, he recognized it as lavender, a scent he had never smelled on another woman. It suited her, though.

Her hands now fisted as she gripped the lapels of his uniform, pulling him closer to her. Now, her breasts pressed against his chest, lighting a fire within him. The need to take more of her overwhelmed him.

Still, he deliberately gentled the kiss, and then he finally broke it. His mouth hovered inches above hers as he asked, "Are you ready to go farther?"

"Yes," she sighed.

Drake's mouth returned to hers, his kisses harder and more in-sistent. Though she was a novice, the duchess was picking up things nicely. He allowed his tongue to outline the shape of her mouth, feeling her tremble against him as he did so. Then slowly, he moved it back and forth against the seam of her mouth, urging her to open to him.

When she understood what he wanted of her, she did so, and he slipped his tongue inside her mouth, tasting a sweetness he had never sampled from any other woman. His tongue caressed hers, and she returned the favor, causing his senses to come alive. He began a leisurely exploration of her, enjoying the taste and feel of her in his arms.

Tilting her head back, it allowed him to deepen the kiss as he claimed more of her. He lost himself in it. Lost track of time. All Drake knew was her mouth. Her taste. The feel and scent of her.

He finally ended the kiss, looking down at her, seeing both the dazed expression he had put on her face and how her eyes were now a darker shade of blue.

Dark because of the desire he had awakened in her.

"That . . . why . . . I have no words, Captain. That was the most moving experience of my life."

He smoothed her hair. "That is only the tip of the iceberg, Duchess. We have many more avenues to explore regarding kissing."

Hesitation filled her eyes, and he realized she must have regretted what had already passed between them. After all, she was a duchess of the realm, one of the highest-ranking members of society, while he was an orphan from the streets, a man who didn't even recall his own birth name.

Releasing her, he stood. "I am sorry if I took things too far, Your Grace," he said formally.

She shot to her feet, capturing his wrist with her fingers. "No, do not go," she pleaded. "I am sorry I am so inexperienced. I fear I did not please you enough."

"What?" he asked incredulously, seeing she wasn't trying to rid herself of him. That it was her own feelings of inadequacy causing the sudden awkwardness between them.

He placed his hands on her shoulders, squeezing lightly. "You are perfect, Duchess," he said firmly. "You caught on quickly to my lesson in kissing. I look forward to spending more time with you—if you will allow me to do so."

A radiant smile, brighter than the sun, lit her beautiful face. "I want to spend more time with you, Captain Andrews. I want to learn the secrets you can teach me."

He returned her smile. "Then if we are to spend more intimate time together, I believe you should call me Drake."

CHAPTER THREE

D INAH SHOOK HER head at Captain Andrews' suggestion. "No, my dear Captain, that would simply be inappropriate. We do not know each other well enough to address one another by our Christian names."

His eyes twinkled at her. "I already think we know one another fairly well, Duchess," he said, his lips twitching in amusement.

She felt the heat spring to her cheeks, knowing they burned a bright red now.

"I suppose I could reconsider your request," she said primly, the thought of the kisses they had exchanged—and those to come—filling her mind. "My given name is Dinah."

"Dinah," he echoed. "I quite like it. It suits you well. It is feminine, and yet it shows the strength you possess."

"You believe I am strong?" she asked. "No one has ever said that to me before."

He took her hands in his. "Then they were fools. Or unobservant idiots. You entered a marriage with a very powerful man at a tender age, Dinah. You have birthed four daughters and raised them, along with your two nieces. You have run the duke's household efficiently. Although I only met your girls for a brief time at Shadowcrest, they all were polite and seemed quite accomplished. I know you did that all on your own, with no help from anyone else, least of all your husband."

"I did it because they were mine," she told him. "Because I loved them. I have always wanted the best for them. As for my marriage? I knew what was expected of me beyond providing an heir apparent. I have managed Seaton's households and did quite a bit of entertaining while he was alive. He never acknowledged the fact that the events I planned came off seamlessly."

"He was not worthy of you," Captain Andrews assured her. "I doubt many men would be. But for a short while, I would like to try to give you what you need. To acknowledge your beauty and strength. To provide a small escape for you."

"I appreciate that more than you could ever know. Admittedly, it was hard for me to ask this of you. Despite the kisses we have exchanged, we are still, in effect, strangers to one another."

Even as she said those words, though, Dinah felt she did know this man. That he was good, down to his very core.

He squeezed her hands. "Then if we are to get to know one another on a more intimate level, I insist that you call me Drake."

"It is such a strong-sounding name. Commanding. For a strong man. I do not refer simply to your physicality. I know you worked your way up from the lowest position on a ship to that of captaining *Vesta*. That speaks volumes to your character. Your determination. Your leadership and integrity."

"Thank you for those compliments, Dinah," he said, his steady gaze causing tingles to shoot through her. "Being a ship's captain is a lonely business, I have found. I want to have a rapport with my crew, yet I cannot become overly friendly with them, or they will not respect my command. When James was the captain of *Vesta* and I served as his first mate, we at least had each other."

"Do you now have a capable first mate?" she asked.

"Denby is most efficient, but he understands that even between a captain and first mate, a certain formality must be observed. I respect Denby, and he respects me. But as to confiding in him, as I did in

James and he did in me? That will not happen. I was on my own during my maiden voyage as captain. I suppose it will remain that way in the future. I doubt I will ever be as close to any man as I was to James."

She squeezed his fingers. "Do not speak of it as if your friendship is in the past, Drake. James still views you as the brother he never had."

He smiled ruefully. "While he will always be the brother of my heart, James is now a duke. He moves in a society I will never know, much less understand. Yes, I do hope to see him while I am in England. Before I leave on my next voyage. But with us no longer being in proximity on a daily basis, our closeness is bound to fade over time." He shrugged. "Besides, I heard he wed Mrs. Grant."

"Come. Sit again with me. Let us continue our conversation," Dinah urged.

They returned to the settee, and a small thrill shot through her when Drake took her hand and threaded his fingers through hers.

"Sophie is the most remarkable woman I have ever encountered," she informed him. "She came from the *ton*, her circumstances similar to my own. Her father wed her to a much older man. Though Josiah Grant was not a member of Polite Society, he was immensely wealthy. Grant built Neptune Shipping Lines from the ground up, and he taught Sophie everything about the business until she was running it before his passing."

"I recall meeting with her after her husband was gone. She was certainly informed and knowledgeable about all aspects of the shipping business."

"There was some gossip after James wed Sophie. Women of the *ton* simply do not work, much less run a business empire. But Sophie is terribly kind and ever so sweet. She won over a great deal of Polite Society, just as she did James and our family."

"The fact that she had faith in me—and made me captain of *Vesta* with such little experience—surprised me. Of course, I know James had recommended me to her, but she took a great risk putting one of her leading trading vessels in my care."

"She is carrying their first child now," Dinah revealed.

Drake smiled, a smile so sunny and genuine, that she realized just how false the smiles of the gentlemen she had been seeing this Season truly were.

"Yes, Mr. Barnes informed me of that happy news," he said. "James must be over the moon. He found his family—and now he is creating one of his own with his duchess. I am to go see them at Shadowcrest."

"When?"

"Before I came here, I reported to the Neptune Shipping offices, where I met with Mr. Barnes. He told me he travels to Kent every week or so to consult with Her Grace regarding business matters. He is preparing a report, which will include the results of my trading expedition. Barnes knows I want to see James, and so I am to take this report to Shadowcrest when I visit."

"Perhaps we might travel to Kent together," she suggested, thinking it might be easier to be alone with him in the country than here in town.

"Don't you have social obligations you have committed to?" he asked.

Dinah shrugged. "I am but one individual, a widow, at that. The Season is more for gentlemen reviewing the women on the Marriage Mart."

He looked at her knowingly. "Have you placed yourself on this so-called Marriage Mart this year, Dinah, now that you are a widow?"

"I will admit that I have been open to the idea of marriage again. I have attended many social events and received callers each afternoon."

His brow furrowed. "Are you serious about any of them? I would not want to overstep if you are."

"No," she said frankly. "While I believe there are more than a few I could enter into marriage with, it would merely be a pleasant union. Not one of passion. Or love."

She hesitated a moment and then added, "I am hoping you will show me what passion is, Drake. What it means to feel desire and fulfill it. If I have that knowledge, perhaps I could make a match with an affable gentleman and bring something to my second marriage that was lacking in my first."

He frowned a moment, and then his features relaxed again.

"Just how far do you want to take our relationship, Dinah? I want transparency between us."

She swallowed, hesitant to voice her needs. But then she recalled he had complimented her, telling her she possessed a strength which had never been acknowledged.

Meeting his gaze, she said, "I want to know all of it. I need you in my bed, Drake. I want you to show me what truly can occur between a man and a woman. I know there are mysteries in the marriage bed which were never revealed to me. I yearn to lose my ignorance and discover them in detail."

He cradled her cheek with his palm. "Then I am more than willing to embark upon an affair with you. I will show you these things, Dinah. I suspect you possess a very sensual nature. One which you have buried deeply, having no release for it. I will teach you to acknowledge it and not be ashamed of it. I plan to enlighten you about what occurs between a man and a woman who are open to exploring one another."

She wet her lips nervously. "I know you have years of experience. You have said as much to me."

His thumb caressed her cheek. "I do know how to please a woman, Dinah. I plan to please you in many ways."

She desperately wanted him to kiss her again.

"You do?" he asked, looking amused.

A hot blush stained her cheeks. "Did I voice that aloud?"

Laughter rumbled deep within his chest. "I believe you did, Duchess. You know a little about kissing now. Kiss *me*."

"You want me . . . to kiss you . . . first?"

"I do. Show me that you desire me. Because I want you to kiss me. Very much so."

She cradled his face with her hands. Slowly, she pulled him down to her, until their lips met. It was as if electricity shot through her. This man made her feel things no other man ever had.

Dinah pushed her fingers into his dark, thick hair, holding tightly as she increased the pressure of her mouth on his. She broke the kiss and immediately kissed him again. And again. Something began filling her, which had to be desire. Her breasts tingled. Her core tightened. She imitated his previous actions, using the tip of her tongue to run along the seam of his mouth, teasing it open.

Boldly pushing her tongue inside his mouth, she found his and caressed it, hearing a groan come from him. Immediately, a sense of power flooded her. *Her* touch had caused that sound to emit from him.

And she wanted to hear it again.

Dinah tightened her grip on him, and thus began the war between their tongues as they fought for control. She instinctively understood there would be no losers in this battle. Only winners.

She kissed him with everything she possessed, feeling her breasts swell and grow heavy as she did. She longed for his touch there and decided he would have no objection if she demanded it.

Releasing her hold on him, she found his hand. Taking his wrist, she brought his hand to her breast. Breaking their kiss, she murmured, "Touch me. Here."

Drake kissed her again, both his hands going to her breasts, kneading them until she whimpered. Then he tweaked the nipples, causing hot desire to flood her. She broke the kiss and gazed at him, asking, "Will you kiss my breasts?"

He smiled at her. "You are learning, Duchess," he said, his voice husky.

He dipped one hand into the bodice of her gown, lifting and freeing her breast. His callused fingers brushed over it, teasing her nipple until it stood taut. Then he dipped his head, and his mouth was on her, sucking hard, causing her core to pound violently.

Drake feasted on her breast, sucking, laving, nipping at it playfully. His teeth grazed the nipple, making her shudder.

Lifting his head, he said, "I shouldn't neglect your other breast."

He freed the untouched one, dining upon it until Dinah writhed. She had wrapped her arms about him, pressing his head close to her, her entire body coming alive. Never had she felt such need pouring through her.

Then he stopped, raising his head, a satisfied look on his handsome features. He slipped her breasts back into place and took her hands in his, lifting them and kissing her knuckles.

"You asked me for that," he said. "That is a very big step, Dinah. To understand what you need and ask your lover for it."

She gave him a timid smile. "It was not as hard as I thought it might be." Pausing, she added, "But I find myself greedy, Drake. I want more. So much more."

He laughed heartily. "Then you shall have more, Duchess."

Drake rose. "I have overstayed my welcome." He reached for a sandwich and gobbled it down in one bite.

He proceeded to do the same with four others, washing them down with his cold cup of tea.

Grinning at her, he said, "I hope your cook will be satisfied."

Whipping out his handkerchief, he wrapped three of the scones in it before placing it in his pocket.

Dinah stood, reluctant to let him go. "When will I see you again?" she asked urgently. "Would you like to stay for dinner?"

"Are you having guests?" he asked.

"No. I was just going to have a light meal before I left for a ball."

She brightened. "Would you care to escort me to it? You look incredibly handsome in your captain's uniform. I would be proud to be on your arm."

Drake shook his head. "No. For one thing, the only dance I know is a sailor's jig. I can't be a part of your world, Dinah, and I refuse to keep you from it. Go to your ball tonight. I can call upon you again. Perhaps tomorrow we could take tea together again."

The thought of not seeing him until this time tomorrow caused a deep sadness to run through her.

"I will skip the ball," she told him.

He cocked an eyebrow at her. "Despite what you told me earlier, I believe you would be missed. By several gentlemen, at the very least."

"Possibly by a few. They will most likely call on me tomorrow afternoon to see why I was absent."

This time, she took his hands in hers. "Stay, Drake. Dine with me this evening. We can go from there."

"If that is what you wish, Duchess, then I will do as you ask."

Dinah hoped by the end of this night that Drake Andrews would be in her bed.

CHAPTER FOUR

F OR THE FIRST time in his life, Drake played a dangerous game.
One with his heart.

He had never become emotionally involved with any woman—
and he had had his share of them for over two decades. James had
teased him over the years about being a ladies' man. How his good
looks and athletic frame appealed to women of all ages and nationali-
ties. Drake had never had to chase after a woman. Ever. They all came
to him, no matter where he was in the world.

Yet he had come to this townhouse because of the Duchess of
Seaton. The one woman who had seemed to crawl inside him and stay
with him. And that was only after meeting her on two occasions.
Admittedly, that second time he had spent several hours in her
company, first at Shadowcrest and then on the journey back to
London as he took her to nurse his injured friend.

His gut told him that he should not have come here today. Mr.
Barnes had already informed him that James and his wife were in the
country. Drake would see his friend and employer within a week and
learn of when he would next sail the seven seas. But he had come to
the ducal townhouse for one reason alone.

To see the woman who had continued to haunt his dreams.

Dinah Strong was fascinating to him. An elegant lady of the *ton*,
and yet one who seemed as comfortable with him as she would be in

the presence of the King of England. The fact that she had been taken with him, too, only fed the growing need within him. Need for her. When she asked him to share his knowledge of intimate acts with her, he knew he was playing with fire. Yet he'd stayed anyway. Kissing her. Touching her. Desire filling him.

Nothing good could come of this brief affair. At least for him. For Dinah, he only hoped he could gift her with the tools which would make lovemaking an earthshattering experience for her. She was a woman who had been left on her own far too long. She was still young and deserved to find happiness after being made to wed a man who had tried to treat her no better than a brood mare.

On his part, he must temper his expectations. She would be a novice, so he doubted she would affect him much physically. At least, that is what he planned. He was determined to keep his emotional distance, so that his heart might remain intact.

Because he was dangerously close to losing it to her.

Drake was aware there could be no future for them. They walked in completely different worlds. He earned his living, often doing as much physical labor as the sailors onboard his ship. Since he no longer had James' companionship, Drake had turned into a loner. While he enjoyed being in charge and all the responsibilities which came with captaining a sea vessel, he could never be a part of a crew again. He had tried to fill the emptiness inside him at various ports of call, with women whose names he would never remember and whose faces now blurred.

Embarking upon an affair with Dinah Strong was certainly playing with fire. They could never appear together outside this house. His obvious, inferior rank would have the gossips in the *ton* raking Dinah over the coals. He would not allow her to suffer in such a manner. He was also cognizant that she still had two daughters and two nieces to bring out to Polite Society, and was savvy enough to understand that any gossip affecting the mother would trickle down to her girls. That was the reason he had denied her when she had asked him to escort her to tonight's ball. She could not afford to be seen with him.

He resolved to be discreet. To introduce the duchess into the ways of lovemaking, enough so that when she did remarry, she would bring a bit of experience and know enough about her own body to make certain her new husband pleased her.

As for him, he would walk away from their brief time together with a heavy heart—but hopefully beautiful memories.

She rang for a maid to collect the tea tray after he ate the scones he had wrapped in his handkerchief.

"I only hope you will have room for dinner," she teased.

"I was always hungry as a boy," he shared. "I only have a vague impression of my parents and have no idea what they did to earn a living. I do remember there never being enough to eat."

"Was it just the three of you? Or did you have any siblings?"

He frowned. "I can't recall any. That doesn't mean my mother didn't have more. Where we lived, a babe was more likely to die than live."

"Oh, Drake." Dinah placed her hand on his forearm, her touch causing his heart to leap. "I am so sorry you endured such poverty."

"I know my parents did die, though I couldn't tell you how old I was when that happened. I remember trying to wake my father. He didn't move. I know my mother was sick, too, but the details are scrambled in my head. It was so long ago. I do recall our landlord coming and physically booting me out the door."

Her eyes brimmed with tears. "How awful. And here I complained to you about having to wed a duke and live in the lap of luxury."

"You went through your own trials, Dinah," he comforted. "No less than mine. Only different."

"How did you survive, living on the streets?"

"I stole when I could. Small items I could sell. I dug through rubbish, looking for anything edible. It was almost a blessing when I was taken by a sailor and forced aboard a ship. At least I had honest work to do and enough food to fill my belly."

She stroked his sleeve absently. The gesture brought him comfort, something he hadn't expected from her.

"James has told me that you saved him. That you nursed him back to health after a sailor savagely beat him."

"I did," he said softly, thinking of that long ago time and the small boy who had been brought to sea, the same as he had been. "He became a younger brother to me—and then my friend. We have spent thousands of hours in one another's company. Not just working. Oftentimes, we read the same books and discussed them as we sat on deck, staring up at the stars in the night sky."

"You like to read?" she asked, clearly surprised.

"I do. A fellow sailor taught me, and I took to reading much as I did to life at sea itself."

He mentioned some of the books which were favorites of his, and she had read several of them. They talked about books for a good hour, as if they were two old friends coming together after a long time apart.

"I must say I am surprised you are so well read," Dinah said. "I suppose I didn't think of the average sailor as a reader. Then again, you are not average in any way."

He ignored her compliment. "And I suppose I thought well-brought up ladies of Polite Society only did needlework and played a musical instrument."

"I do both—and quite well," she said saucily, causing him to laugh. "I also enjoy gardening and arranging flowers. Lyric takes after me in that respect. Georgina and Mirella are accomplished pianists, playing much better than I ever did, but they practice all the time. I do like to ride and taught all the girls how to do so. Pippa and Effie are the most proficient in the saddle. Allegra is one for long walks. She and I have enjoyed hours in one another's company, walking from one end of

Shadowcrest to the other."

"You have been a shining example to all those girls. I am sorry your husband and brother-in-law did not value females."

She snorted. "Polite Society does not harbor fond feelings for females, Drake. Every man wants a male heir and plenty of spares. It is the rare man who does not mind having daughters, much less one who pays attention to them."

"It was the duke's loss, Dinah, with him ignoring you and all the girls you made together."

"You are right," she agreed. "Seaton is the one who missed out. James will be a much better duke than his father ever was, as well as a kind, loving father."

When it was time to dine, she said, "I do not see the point of us going to the dining room. It seats thirty-six. Custom would have us eating at opposite ends. I choose not to shout down the table at you. I will have Powell place us in the winter parlor instead."

She rang for the butler and gave him those instructions. Minutes later, Powell returned, telling them dinner was ready to be served.

Drake offered her his arm, and she accepted it. He liked feeling possessive of her, having her close, her hand on his sleeve. Still, he refused to allow his heart to soften toward her. He would make love to her, multiple times, showing her what she needed to know to make herself and a partner happy, keeping her at arm's length.

Because if he did let her into his heart, it would be torn asunder when he left England.

The winter parlor was a very cozy, intimate room, with a table set for two. Drake seated Dinah and then himself.

The butler supervised a footman, who poured wine for them both, while another brought a tureen, filling their bowls with a vegetable soup.

Dinah thanked the footman and then told the butler, "Powell, we can simply serve ourselves since it is only the two of us this evening.

No sense in having the staff wait on us."

Drake nearly guffawed when the butler looked pained at the instructions. "Very well, Your Grace. If you are certain."

"I am, Powell. Thank you very much," she said kindly—but firmly—in effect, dismissing the butler and the other servants.

When they left, closing the door behind them, she spooned a bite of soup into her mouth. "Oh, it is so nice to eat in private. With it being only me in residence, I often take my morning and evening meals in my rooms."

"Do they always stand and watch while you eat?" he asked.

"Yes. Part of their service is to always be on duty during meals, in order to anticipate any needs. It can be awkward at times, though, especially if you wish to have a private discussion with someone."

"Never fear, Duchess. I shall serve you. I also look forward to anticipating your needs," he said, waggling his brows playfully, causing her to laugh. He liked her laugh. From such a dainty person, it was a rich, deep laugh, showing she had a side to her that he believed wasn't often shared with others.

They worked their way through the meal, dining on a cabbage pudding and roasted veal. For dessert, he was happy to see baked apple tarts.

He bit into a tart and sighed. "My compliments to your cook, Dinah. No wonder you do not wish to hurt her feelings. She is a true gem."

"I am glad you have enjoyed the meal, Drake."

"*Vesta's* cook gives us simple fare. Actually, we eat the same, few dishes over and over. We also take advantage of being at sea and eat quite a bit of fish. Frankly, I was happy not to see a fish dish appear at this meal."

She laughed again, causing his blood to run hot. Everything about her spoke to him.

He could not wait to drive her to orgasm.

They finished their tarts, and she rang for a maid to clear the small table.

"Would you pour more wine for me, Captain Andrews?" she asked as the maid emptied the table.

"Of course, Your Grace," he said formally. "It is quite good."

"It is French. Sometimes, I feel unpatriotic drinking it, but it was bought long ago, before our countries were at war."

The maid left, rolling the cart from the room and shutting the door.

"Would you like to move to the settee while we sip our wine?" she asked.

Doing his best to sound like a cultured gentleman, Drake said, "That would be most enjoyable."

Dinah burst out laughing. "I cannot remember the last time I have enjoyed someone's company so much, Drake."

He clinked his wine glass against hers. "I quite agree, Duchess."

They both drank deeply of the wine, and then Drake took the glass from her hand, setting it down along with his own. He turned to her, seeing the sky blue of her eyes had darkened again.

She wanted him. He wanted her. Yet he wanted to prolong their evening—and a final coupling. Instead, he would give her another lesson, one which he hoped would drive her to the point of ecstasy.

Drake slipped his hand about her nape, guiding her to him. Their lips met, and he kissed her softly for several minutes, feeling the sexual tension build between them. Then he slid his tongue back and forth across her plump, bottom lip. She easily opened to him, knowing what to expect now.

So he decided to befuddle her—and increase that tension.

He sank his teeth into her bottom lip. Not hard, but it surprised her. She made a squeak, and he licked the place, soothing it with his tongue. He nipped her again, his heart racing, and it took him off-guard when she did the same to him. The love bite caused instant desire to shoot through him, and he lifted her into his lap, his tongue sweeping inside her mouth. He tasted the wine they had shared, along with the unique taste which was all Dinah. All Duchess. Everything he wanted.

They greedily kissed, his pulse racing, his hands holding her waist, his thumbs caressing her ribcage. Dinah made little noises of appreciation as they kissed.

Then she wriggled on his lap, and he nearly spent, then and there.

Breaking the kiss, he said, "Easy, love. You moving like that, well, it does things to me."

Her eyes danced with mischief. "Good things, I hope."

"Things meant for later," he said sternly. "But I have something wonderful in store for you."

"Oh, do tell," she teased.

He smiled wickedly. "I am more about showing than telling, Duchess."

His hand slipped beneath her gown, finding a trim ankle and a most shapely calf. He moved his hand against the silk of her stocking, hearing her breath catch.

"That feels wonderful, Drake," she told him.

He laughed softly. "Oh, I have yet to begin."

Her lips parted, and he pulled her to him again, his tongue plunging deep inside her, craving the taste of her. His fingers grazed her knee and then thigh before finding the seam of her sex. He danced a finger along it, moving back and forth. Dinah stilled, breaking the kiss. He saw curiosity in her eyes.

As he pushed a finger inside her, she whimpered, biting her lip. "Are you supposed to do something like that?" she asked worriedly.

"What a man and woman do together is between them. There *are* no rules, Duchess. Only pleasure to be had."

"Truly?" she asked, her brow furrowing.

"Truly," he assured her, beginning to stroke her deeply.

She almost came off his lap, and he chuckled. "Easy, love. Close your eyes."

"All right," she said reluctantly, doing so.

Drake watched her face as his finger continue to caress her. He slid another one into her, and she sucked in another loud breath. Her breathing became fast and shallow as she began to move against him. He smiled, knowing this would be her first orgasm.

And he was the one to give it to her.

"Oh. Oh. Oh!" she moaned, breathing even faster.

"Move as you wish," he told her softly.

She did so as he increased the speed of his strokes. Her hips began rocking, her eyelids fluttering, sweet sounds coming from her perfect, rosebud mouth. She grew louder, and he did not want anyone listening at the keyhole to ascertain what they were up to. He covered her mouth with his, kissing her deeply, his tongue now mimicking what his fingers did.

Then she stiffened. Began rocking violently. Murmuring into his mouth. He rubbed her nape with one hand, stilling his hand so she moved against it as he held it in place.

A sigh, long, drawn-out, and a terribly satisfying sound came from her. Her eyes opened, and he saw how dark they now were. He caressed her a final time and withdrew his fingers, bringing them to his mouth and licking them.

Her eyes widened in surprise. "*What* are you doing?"

"Tasting you," he said matter-of-factly. "But there is another way I can do that, as well. A way you will enjoy tremendously, Duchess."

Easing her off his lap, he knelt before her, pushing her gown and the garments beneath it up, bunching them about her waist. She was bare to him, though she wore silk stockings that came to her knee, tied with tiny bows to hold them up.

Drake took off her slippers and brought her feet to the settee, planting them flat.

Her face flamed. "This is . . . so . . . inappropriate," she managed to say.

He glanced down at her and then up until their gazes met. "You are beautiful, Dinah. Everywhere. And after a small taste of you, I must have more."

He lowered his head between her opened thighs, bracing his hands on her knees to keep her from trying to close them. Her scent already filled his nostrils, and Drake moved close, inhaling deeply. Then he licked the length of her sex, hearing her cry out in surprise. Unfortunately, he couldn't be in two places at once. If any servant was listening at the door, he or she would now get an earful.

With his only aim to bring her pleasure, Drake plunged his tongue inside her. She squeaked, a sweet, charming sound. He held her knees firmly as his tongue moved in and out of her, relishing her sweet juices, causing her hips to rise and her body to writhe. He feasted on her as he never had another woman, taking, taking, taking more and more, losing himself in her.

Her orgasm erupted with a vengeance, causing her to cry out his name. He quickly moved from her core to her mouth, pressing his body against her rocking one, his tongue finding hers and mating with it. The kiss went on and on, as did her orgasm.

Then she went completely limp, her hands falling away from where they had clutched him. He broke the kiss, seeing she was completely drained.

It gave him satisfaction like none he had ever experienced.

"What did you do to me?" Dinah asked. "I went to the heavens and beyond. I had no idea my body could feel such a thing." She met his gaze. "And where you kissed me! And then when we kissed . . ." Her voice trailed off.

"You could taste yourself," he said. "You have a unique taste, different from any other woman, Duchess." He licked his lips. "Perhaps I should taste you again."

She shook her head. "No. You might kill me, Drake. I have already had that extraordinary feeling twice in the matter of a few minutes. I might not survive it again so soon."

He sat beside her again, slipping his arm about her, drawing her into his chest. Dinah rested her cheek against his heart.

"I had no idea something like that even existed," she said, her voice fading.

"Sleep, Duchess," he commanded. "I will be here when you awake."

He glanced down, seeing her eyelids flutter a few times before they stilled.

The Dowager Duchess of Seaton lay nestled in his arms. Sleeping with a smile on her face, one he had put there. He should be happy that he had been so successful in bringing her into such a new experience. One which she would never forget. He had felt the magnitude of her two orgasms and knew how powerfully they had affected her.

Unfortunately, he had also been affected. In a way which now ruined him.

Because Drake had fallen in love with a woman he could never call his own.

CHAPTER FIVE

DINAH AWOKE, WRAPPED in a delicious warmth. Before she opened her eyes, she realized it was not the bedclothes, but Drake Andrews who warmed her. She lay in his arms, her eyes remining closed so she could relish the feel of his hard body encircling hers. She had never felt as safe as she did in this moment.

What he had done to her was simply incredible. She knew Pippa and Georgina had wed for love, and that their husbands now cared for her daughters in such a fashion. It made her happy to realize her twins were settled with such good, loving men. She wanted the same for her other daughters and her nieces, as well.

And she wanted it for herself.

Drake stirred feelings within her which she had not known could exist. Dinah knew he would continue to open her eyes to all manner of sensual things in the short time they would have together. She had always been practical in nature. The sea captain would only be in England for a brief while. She could not grow overly fond of him. Nor attach herself to him, for he would be gone before she knew it. Besides, as he had pointed out to her, they came from vastly different worlds. Even if she could convince him they might have a future together, it would affect her own girls' futures. Dinah had worked too hard raising her family, and she could not risk her reputation by becoming publicly involved with Captain Andrews. She wanted good matches for her girls. Hopefully, the four would make love matches as her twins had.

But for now, she would enjoy the limited time she had with Drake.

Lazily, she stretched, opening her eyes, feeling his arms tighten slightly about her.

"Did I sleep for very long?" she asked him.

"Barely two hours," he informed her.

Reluctantly, she sat up, pushing away from his hard, muscular body. "I am sorry I held you hostage during that time, Drake. I know you must have other things to do while you are ashore for a brief while."

He smiled at her, a wistful smile that caused tenderness to rise within her. "I was happy to spend the time with you, Dinah. I do have obligations which must be seen to, though."

"You will call tomorrow, won't you?" she asked anxiously.

He shook his head. "No, I have been away from my ship too long. There are things I neglected to do today that must be taken care of tomorrow."

"I am sorry I kept you from your duties, Captain Andrews." She hesitated. "Will you have any time to spend with me before you depart?"

She saw hesitation in his eyes and understood something had changed between them. What, she did not know, but it seemed he was reluctant to continue being her guide into the art of lovemaking.

Standing, Dinah tamped down the vast array of emotions swirling within her. "I understand that I have asked the impossible of you, Captain. I never should have been as brazen as I was, practically demanding that you initiate me into the ways of lovemaking. I do thank you for what you showed me today. You are under no obligation to call upon me again."

He rose, one hand coming to cradle her cheek. "I do not regret a moment of the time we had today. And if you are still willing, I will teach you what you need to know so that in your next marriage, you can be more satisfied physically, if not actually happier."

Her pulse began to pound. "You really do not need to do that," she told him. "I understand it is a commitment of time on your part because I am such a novice. You must have other women you wish to see. Old friends you wish to call upon. Business to attend to."

"Anything I have to do fades when compared to wanting to spend time with you, Duchess. We can be together some of tomorrow if you wish. I will make that happen."

While she yearned to be with him physically, she truly wanted to learn more about the man before her.

"Would you take me to Gunter's?" she asked.

He frowned. "I am not familiar with this establishment."

Dinah chuckled. "Oh, it is a favorite of mine. They serve the most marvelous ices."

"Ices? What are those?"

She explained to him what ices were and told him a few of her favorite flavors. "You must try one. I know you will like it."

He gazed intently at her. "That would mean being seen together in public."

"I know," she said quickly. "I have no objection to it—unless you do."

Drake looked at her longingly, and she had the feeling he was waging a battle within himself.

Finally, he said, "What time should I call upon you?"

"How about one o'clock tomorrow afternoon? Would that give you time to handle the business you must attend to?"

"I will make it happen."

He bent, his lips softly brushing against hers.

Lifting his head, he said, "Good night, Dinah."

Drake moved away from her, opening the door to the winter parlor. She watched him go, thinking what a fine figure he cut in his captain's uniform.

She took a seat again, contemplating how she might sneak him up to her bedchamber. Servants were everywhere in the household. She wasn't certain if she would be up to the task. Like it or not, she cared for the good opinion of the servants. Would they think less of her if they knew she coupled with a sinfully handsome sea captain?

Dinah stood, heading to her bedchamber. When she arrived, her maid waited for her, as did the ballgown she was to have worn to tonight's event.

Letty rose. "I knew you had a guest for dinner, Your Grace, but I didn't know you wouldn't go to tonight's ball. I kept the gown out, ready in case you changed your mind."

"The ball started long ago, Letty. It is too late for me to go. Besides, I find myself rather tired this evening. I think I have been going to too many events. I may cut back on my appearances at them."

The maid tried—and failed—to hide her astonishment and said, "Of course, Your Grace."

"I also may make a short visit to Shadowcrest within the next week," she informed the girl. "I have a few things to put into motion regarding the house party I am planning for the twins. I also miss the girls terribly and would like to see them."

Letty smiled. "I know those girls mean the world to you. Just give the word, and I'll have your things packed in no time."

The servant helped Dinah undress and prepare for bed. She lay awake after Letty left for a long time, reliving every moment she had been with Drake Andrews.

>>>><<<<

DINAH WAS WAITING in the drawing room when Powell informed her Captain Andrews had arrived.

"Have the barouche prepared," she told the butler. "Captain Andrews and I will be going to Gunter's."

"Yes, Your Grace," Powell said, leaving the drawing room. Moments later, the butler escorted her guest in, announcing him.

She rose as Drake crossed the room. He took her hands in his, lifting them and kissing them.

"You look well today, Your Grace," he said, releasing her hands.

"You do, as well, Captain. I hope you were able to attend to the business at hand."

"Last evening and this morning were quite busy," he told her, taking the seat beside her. "I did hear from Mr. Barnes. His report will be completed much sooner than he expected, most like by mid-afternoon tomorrow. I think I will travel to Shadowcrest the following morning to share the report with Her Grace, as well as visit with James."

He said nothing about her accompanying him, and Dinah was afraid to ask, thinking he might have changed his mind about her going with him to Kent.

"I am having the barouche readied to take us to Gunter's. We may eat in it or go inside."

"Eat . . . in a vehicle?" He frowned. "Is that even done?"

She laughed merrily. "It is only done at Gunter's. It is quite the thing to drive up to Berkeley Square and have a runner appear from Gunter's to hear your request. Many people in the *ton* find it pleasant to sit outside as they eat their ices."

"Interesting."

"Of course, we can go inside if you wish. It is one of the few places in town where a gentleman may escort a lady and they can dine together. Their sandwiches rival those of our cook's, and their pastries are a delight."

"Dinah, are you certain that you wish to be seen with me in public? I don't want my presence to affect your reputation in any harmful way."

"It is merely an ice we are sharing," she assured him. "And you are a great friend of the duke's. No one will think anything of it."

Powell appeared, informing her the barouche was ready. Drake escorted her outside, handing her up into the open-air vehicle, and taking the seat opposite her. She hid her disappointment, wishing he had sat next to her, but knowing it was more proper for him to sit where he was.

The coachman took up the reins, and they traveled through the busy streets of London. Dinah knew after missing last night's ball that she would most likely have numerous visitors today, seeking to know why she had not been in attendance. She had told Powell that she would not be at home to any visitors today.

Other than Captain Andrews.

They arrived in Berkeley Square, and she had the coachman pull up under a shade tree, telling him he could go and stretch his legs a bit while they enjoyed their ices.

"It is such a pleasant day. I hope you do not mind if we do eat outside."

Drake smiled. "I am happy to do whatever you wish, Your Grace."

A familiar man scurried across the road, dodging traffic to reach them. He stepped up to their vehicle.

"Good afternoon, Your Grace," he greeted. "We have not seen you for a few weeks."

"I had a hankering for one of your ices today. This is Captain Andrews, of the vessel *Vesta*. He has never experienced an ice before."

The man smiled broadly. "Well, Captain, you are in for quite a treat."

Drake looked at her. "Order for me, Your Grace. I will trust in your good taste."

She gave the server her preference, a lavender ice, and then asked for a chocolate one for her companion.

"I will bring them to you shortly, Your Grace," the man promised, hurrying back across the road and disappearing into the shop.

She glanced about, seeing only one other carriage parked at the square at this time, knowing most others were about to make or receive morning calls at this time of the afternoon. Unfortunately, the one carriage belonged to Lady Cowper, one of the most notorious gossips of the *ton*. The countess eyed Dinah and Drake with interest.

"We are an object of speculation," she warned. "Do not look over your shoulder, but Lady Cowper is marching our way."

Moments later, the countess appeared beside their carriage. "Your Grace, I am so surprised to see you out and about."

"Whyever so, Lady Cowper? I thought most members of Polite Society knew I had a fondness for Gunter's ices."

"Well, you were absent from last night's ball." The countess glanced to Drake and back at Dinah, eyeing her knowingly. "Others thought you must have suddenly taken ill since no word was sent to your host and hostess."

"As you can see, I am the picture of good health. Might I introduce Captain Andrews to you, Lady Cowper? He served with my stepson for many years and now captains the very vessel His Grace did at one time. Captain Andrews is a great friend of our family."

"Is that so?" the countess asked pointedly, looking at Drake with interest. "You do realize, Captain, that Their Graces have retired to the country to await the birth of their first child."

Drake gave the woman his most charming smile. "I do, Lady Cowper. I simply called upon Her Grace to see how she fares. I will be journeying to Shadowcrest in a couple of days to visit with Their Graces. As you know, Her Grace is my employer, and I have many things to share with her regarding my most recent voyage. I also look forward to spending time with His Grace. We are as close as brothers."

The countess arched a brow. "Are you?"

"We most certainly are," Drake assured the woman, his blinding smile never faltering. "In fact, Her Grace was just telling me how much she misses her daughters and nieces, who are in Kent."

He turned to her. "If you are eager to see them, Your Grace, I would be happy to escort you to Shadowcrest in order for you to have a short visit with them. I will most likely stay a couple of days before heading back to town."

"Why, that would be lovely, Captain Andrews," Dinah responded. "It would give me a small respite from the Season, and I could also put into motion plans for my upcoming house party."

Lady Cowper perked up. "You are holding a house party, Your Grace?"

"I am, my lady, at the end of the Season. My nieces chose not to make their come-outs this spring when Georgina did, but they are eager for the company of society now. I thought a house party would be the best way to introduce them to a select group of people in a more intimate setting."

When no invitation to Lady Cowper was forthcoming, she nodded brusquely. "I see. Well, give my best to Their Graces when you see them."

The countess turned away, not bothering to say farewell to Drake, whose lips twitched in amusement.

"She seems like a difficult person," he commented. "And I'll wager she's a notorious gossip."

"Lady Cowper will let others know we were seen together," Dinah told him. "She will also let it be known that I am holding a house party for Allegra and Lyric. A very exclusive one, to which Lord and Lady Cowper will not be receiving an invitation."

He laughed. "Don't worry. I don't expect an invitation to it myself. I might already be at sea by that time."

The thought of him gone from her life so soon distressed Dinah, but she was determined not to let him see her despondency.

Instead, she brightened. "Why, I see our ices are coming," she declared.

The runner brought them on a tray, handing her lavender ice to her first, along with a spoon and napkin, and then giving Drake his chocolate one.

"Enjoy," the server called cheerfully, leaving them.

She spooned a bite of ice into her mouth, sighing. "There is nothing like a Gunter's ice on a warm summer's day," she proclaimed.

For his part, Drake took a bite, his eyes lighting in delight. "This is incredible. Easily, the best thing I have ever sampled." Eagerly, he took a second bite.

She watched as Lady Cowper's carriage drove past them. Dinah waved to the countess, who curtly bobbed her head in acknowledgement.

Once the countess had gone, Drake surprised her, moving to sit next to her.

"Do you like the chocolate one?" he asked, dipping his spoon into his ice.

"Very much so."

He brought his spoon to her mouth. "Then try some of mine."

Dinah's heart sped up. She opened her mouth, and he slipped the spoon inside it, lifting it so she got the bite, pulling it from her mouth slowly.

Leaning in, he said, "I wish we weren't in public," his voice low so that the driver couldn't hear. "Because I would like to lick your lips and taste you now."

She shivered. "I would like to do the same," she said softly, her gaze locked on him. "Would you like to try a bite of the lavender?"

"Very much so."

Placing her spoon into the ice, she raised the spoon to his lips. He opened, taking the spoon in, his gaze never leaving hers. Gently, Dinah pulled the spoon but he teased her, holding it tight. She pulled harder, freeing it, flustered now. Not knowing what to do, she dipped the spoon into her ice again and took a bite, knowing the utensil had been inside him moments ago. That knowledge caused her cheeks to heat.

They finished their ices in silence, and the man who had brought the ices to them returned to retrieve the empty dishes.

"Did you enjoy your ices?" he asked.

"Very much so," Drake replied for both of them. "I hope we will come again very soon so that I might sample another flavor."

Drake did not return to his original seat. Instead, he stayed beside her. She caught his scent, a potent mix of sandalwood and something inherently masculine, and forced herself to keep her hands folded in her lap instead of pushing them into his hair and pulling him down for a kiss. To do so in public would end all chances her girls had of making good matches. She must be on alert and behave properly.

Even though this man made her want to do very wicked things with him.

The driver returned, and Dinah told him to take them home. When they arrived, Drake exited the barouche and then handed her down.

"I know how busy you are. Thank you for taking the time to see me."

His eyes gleamed at her. "Do you think you can get rid of me that easily, Duchess?"

"I thought—"

"I think you should ask me if I would like to see your gardens."

She wet her lips. "Would you like to see the gardens, Captain Andrews?"

He smiled, a smile that drew her in. "I thought you would never ask, Your Grace."

CHAPTER SIX

D RAKE HAD NO interest in strolling the gardens. What he was interested in was being alone with Dinah. Without any servant or meddlesome countess interrupting them.

He had thought about her often during the long months at sea, but now she filled his every waking moment. He believed it best to cut all ties with her, yet he had agreed to see her again today, turning up at her doorstep, knowing he was in love with her.

Something he would never tell her.

But he could give them both a gift before they parted and he returned to sea. He could make love with her—and that memory would be what saw him through the decades to come. The question was when they could be alone. And where. It wasn't as if he could saunter up to her bedchamber and spend a night in her bed. Servants talked, and he refused to let gossip about Dinah float amongst the members of the *ton*.

She had talked to him of enjoying the outdoors and gardening. It would be only natural that she would want to show off the gardens to her guest. And there, he hoped he might be able to do more than kiss her.

The butler greeted them as they entered the foyer. "Would you care for any refreshments, Your Grace?"

"No, thank you, Powell. We have just come from having ices at

Gunter's. I did tell Captain Andrews about our gardens, both here and at Shadowcrest." She turned to him, as if she only now had the idea. "Would you care to see the gardens, Captain? My geraniums have proved most hardy, and the sweet peas are especially pretty this year. Oh, and you must view my abutilons. Our gardener did an especially good job protecting them from frost this winter, and now their blooms are quite lovely."

Playing his part, Drake said, "I know little about plants and flowers, Your Grace, but I would love to have you explain about them to me. That is, if you have the time."

She linked her arm through his. "Oh, I will make the time, Captain. There are few things I enjoy talking about as much as the gardens." Dinah looked to the butler. "I am sure we will work up a thirst being in the gardens so long. Please have tea waiting for us at four in the drawing room, Powell."

His eyes cut to the grandfather clock, which chimed the half-hour. That would give them ninety minutes alone before they were expected back.

He planned to make the most of it.

Dinah led him to a small parlor and opened one of the French doors, saying, "This is the quickest way to the gardens."

They exited the house and strolled to the gardens. As they drew near, he picked up the scent of flowers. She paused at the entrance, bending and sniffing.

"This is dianthus," she told him. "It gives off a wonderful aroma of clove."

He bent and inhaled. "It does."

They stepped into the gardens, out of sight, and she hurried him along the path until they reached a gazebo, octagonal in shape, with benches lining several sides. Dinah pulled him up the three stairs to the center and reached high, throwing her arms about his neck and jerking him down for a kiss.

The kiss caught fire instantly, and their tongues warred for control. Drake pinned her against him as he savaged her mouth, the feel of her ample breasts pressing against his chest driving him into a frenzy.

Breaking the kiss, he said, "We may never have the luxury of being in your bedchamber. Will this place do? Might we be interrupted?"

She toyed with the hair at his nape, tugging on it. "No. The gardener and his wife received news of their first grandchild being born yesterday morning. I told them to go and visit the newborn. They will not be back until the day after tomorrow. No one will see us."

"Good," he said, seizing her mouth again, hunger for her consuming him.

They kissed until both were out of breath. He scooped her up and sat on one of the benches. Dinah looped her arms about his neck and kissed his brow. His cheeks. His mouth.

"I need more of you than that," he told her, coming to his feet and setting her on hers.

Drake bent and lifted the hem of her gown, raising it until he pulled it over her head. He laid it across the back of one of the benches, hoping it wouldn't wrinkle. Next, he removed the one petticoat she wore, placing it next to the gown. Then he spun her around, his fingers quickly unlacing her stays. Dinah wriggled from them, and he set the stays on the bench.

He faced her, seeing she now only wore her shift. He could see through the soft, white material the dark areolas of her breasts. The nipples already stood at attention, waiting for his hands and mouth.

He removed his jacket and cravat before unbuttoning his shirt, pulling it over his head. He rested his clothing on another bench.

Turning, he took her hands and placed them on his chest. "Feel me," he commanded. "Move your palms over my chest. My shoulders. My back."

She did so, her eyes taking him in, her mouth pursed in curiosity. Her touch sent wild urges through him, and Drake fought for control.

"You are sculpted, Drake," she marveled. "Like a marble statue come to life. Warm. Muscled."

She tweaked his nipples, and desire surged through him. He caught her, kissing her again, tugging on her hair so that he could deepen the kiss. His cock sprang to life, pressing between them.

Dinah broke the kiss and looked down. As she rubbed her hand against his cock, still covered, he groaned.

"I hope you do not mind me touching you," she said. "I have never done something like this." She unbuttoned his trousers, freeing his cock. "Oh, this is something I have never seen before." She stroked it. "Soft and yet hard."

"I want your touch. Everywhere," he admitted, kissing her hard.

He guided her backward a few steps until her back came to rest against a post. He lifted her hands over her head, capturing her wrists in one hand, placing them against the post, as his other hand kneaded her breast. His mouth took hers, and Drake could taste the lavender ice she had eaten, as well as smell lavender coming off her heated skin.

His fingers rolled her nipple, causing a gasp to come from her. He smiled.

"I am going to touch you as I did last night," he told her, her eyes darkening with desire at his words. "You will like it."

"I know," she whispered.

He raised the chemise high enough until it was out of his way and feathered his fingers along the seam of her sex. She wriggled, trying to free her hands, but he kept them pinned.

Drake pushed two fingers inside her, caressing her deeply. She began moving against the post and his hand as he watched her eyes glaze.

"It is happening again," she said, wonder in her voice. "That pressure. It builds and builds and then spills over, like water breaking through a dam."

"You are wet for me, Duchess," he said, his lips moving against her long, elegant neck, kissing it as his fingers found her nub and circled it.

"Oh! Oh!" she cried.

Whether they were alone or not, he couldn't have her shouting, so his mouth went to hers, covering it. As he kissed her, he brought her to a climax, and she moved against him. Dinah shuddered and stilled.

Now was the time. He released her wrists, and her hands fell to her side.

"Stay on your feet," he ordered. "Lean against the post for support."

She did so as he pushed down his trousers, not bothering to step out of them. Dinah glanced down, her mouth opening as she stared at the size of his swelling cock.

"So, that is what it looks like. Seaton always insisted upon it being dark."

He captured her face in his hands. "I am nothing like Seaton. And you are now with me. This will be different than anything you ever did with him. Nothing will be the same."

Drake took her by the waist, anchoring her, and thrust into her. She clutched his shoulders, her nails digging into them.

"You are definitely wet for me, Duchess."

She shivered at his words.

He began moving in and out of her. She caught his rhythm and responded to it. He lifted her legs, saying, "Wrap them about my waist," and she did. Now, he leaned her against that post, thrusting in and out, driven wild by her lavender scent, burying himself in her soft flesh again and again. His fingers found her nub and he pressed hard against it, circling it, making her pant.

She cried out, her body trembling with the orgasm that racked her body. He felt his own coming and pulled her legs from his waist, setting her on the ground. With one last thrust, he pulled out, spending on the ground, his breath harsh, the blood pounding in his ears.

Her hands captured his face, jerking him down so their lips collided. Dinah kissed him, over and over, and he reveled in each kiss. Love for this woman flowed through him, and he fought the urge to cry to the heavens about it. But even if she came to love him, they could never be together. It was better to leave things unsaid.

She finally broke the kiss, resting her brow against his. "I never knew it could be like that. Good heavens, I birthed four children and not once did getting with child feel like that did."

He chuckled. "There will be no child. I did not spill my seed inside you."

Raising her head, she gazed deeply at him. "I would not mind if a child was the result, Drake. Because I love you."

They were words he would always treasure hearing, but he had to put a stop to this madness.

"Do not fancy yourself in love with me, Dinah. A man and woman can come together and enjoy the pure physicality of the act. Love does not necessarily play a part in lovemaking."

Her gaze never wavered. "Tell me you do not feel as I do. Tell me I am wrong about what is growing between us. Tell me you do not love me."

He opened his mouth, ready to spout the lie—and then knew he couldn't betray her in such a way.

"I do love you, Dinah," he admitted, his breath still coming harshly. "It is wrong of me, but by God, I do."

He kissed her, hard and possessive, not knowing if they would ever have the opportunity to couple together in the future.

Pausing, he said, "But you know why we cannot acknowledge this. I am only here for a short while before I return to sea. I am gone for months—even years—at a time. I am an orphan who cannot even recall his own name, a child born into poverty. You are a leading member of Polite Society, a bloody duchess. Much as I wish things could be different, there is no hope for us, Dinah. None. So do not say those words again, because they already are tearing me apart."

"Oh, Drake," she said softly, bringing her arms about him and clinging to him, her check resting against his bare chest. "What have we done?"

He stroked her hair. "We have done nothing wrong," he assured her. "We were merely two lonely people who came together. I will soon be gone, and we will return to the worlds we each inhabit."

Lifting her head, she told him, "I do not want you to leave. I want you to stay. With me."

"I cannot do that, Duchess," he said, his voice rough with emotion. "I must earn my living. I have finally achieved a dream I never thought would come true. I am captain of my own ship. I belong at sea."

"You belong with me," she said stubbornly.

"No, I could never exist in your world," he said, his heart breaking as he spoke the words. "You are at the highest echelon of British society. You will wed again. Your husband will be from your world."

Tears streamed down her cheeks. "But he will never understand me as you do. He will never make me feel cherished as you have."

"He will. You simply haven't found him yet."

Anger sparked in her blue eyes. "You think I would wish to be with another man after I have been with you? If you believe that, you are sorely mistaken."

She pushed hard at his chest, stepping away, smoothing her chemise and picking up her stays. She slipped into them and fumbled with the laces, out of her sight.

"Here. Let me," he said, glad his fingers had lacing to do—because all they wanted was to skim her satin skin.

She stood stiffly until he finished and then said, "Thank you," in a tight voice.

As she replaced her petticoat and gown, he repaired his own clothing, finally slipping into his fitted jacket. Their eyes met, and he saw yearning in hers, knowing they reflected what was in his own eyes.

"I will not be staying for tea," he said. "It would be unwise. If you can point me to the gate, I can leave from here."

"You are a coward," she said pointedly. "You are running away from me."

"I cannot run *to* you, Dinah," he protested. "I have explained why we could never be together."

Fisting her hands, she rested them on her waist. "You could at least let us enjoy the time we have together. Until you set sail again on *Vesta*." Her chin raised a notch, daring him to challenge her words.

All the fight went out of him. "You are right. We love one another. We should make the most of what little time we have together. I promise to spend as much time with you as I can, Dinah, before I am given my next assignment. It means I will leave with a broken heart— but I'd be a bloody fool to walk away from you before I have to."

She collapsed against him, and he held her close, stroking her hair, murmuring soothing words of nonsense to her.

Being with her—and then having to leave her—would break him.

But Drake would rather be broken than lose any time with her.

CHAPTER SEVEN

DINAH ACCEPTED THE hand Drake offered, and stepped into the carriage James had left in town for her use. Drake entered after she did, sitting opposite her.

They had spent almost every waking moment together the past two days. He had made love to her again in the gazebo. In the conservatory. Twice after dining in the winter parlor. Another two times in the drawing room. They had yet to be together in a bed.

She hoped they would be able to accomplish that while at Shadowcrest.

He had arrived this morning with the sheaf of papers to take to his employer. Mr. Barnes had prepared several reports for his employer and was now entrusting Drake to meet with the duchess and discuss them with her. Dinah had sent word that the two of them would be arriving at Shadowcrest around noon today. She only wondered if they would make love in the carriage on the way there. They would have to stop and change the horses about two-thirds of the way there, and that might prove to be an inconvenience to their lovemaking.

Now they had admitted their love for one another, she knew the heartache which lay ahead would be impossible. Still, she put off thinking about a day without Drake in it. In such a short time, he had become such a huge part of her life.

Dinah had sent her regrets to various hostesses, explaining she missed her girls and was traveling to Shadowcrest for several days. She had not attended a *ton* event since Drake had appeared in her drawing room, so she could only guess at the gossip Lady Cowper spread. It didn't matter to her one whit, though. What she had found with Drake was what she had been searching for the entire Season. No gentleman of the *ton* had his dashing looks, charm, and intelligence. She had told herself she was open to wedding again, but her heart told her no man of Polite Society held a candle to Drake Andrews.

Between bouts of lovemaking, where she had learned all manner of things and allowed her lover to place her in a variety of positions, they had talked. Really talked. Dinah had never had such deep conversations with anyone. Certainly not her parents, whom she had rarely seen growing up, much less her husband, whom she saw even less. The friends she had amongst the *ton* were in actuality familiar acquaintances. None of what she discussed with them compared to her talks with Drake.

They spoke of history, a topic both of them were fond of. Since he was so well-read, they had enjoyed arguing over various characters in Shakespeare's plays. He did not know much about politics, a topic which fascinated Dinah, and so she had explained to him issues of the day which Parliament dealt with.

For his part, he explained what life at sea was like. How he had first learned to navigate by the stars. He went into detail about the various positions he'd held on ships and the responsibilities of a first mate and captain. She could have listened to him for hours. She did not know if what he said interested her because it was interesting—or if she merely enjoyed hearing about it because Drake was the one telling her these things.

Regardless, she had come to know him better than anyone else, besides her girls. She had spent years raising them and could almost predict how they would react in any situation. Still, she wondered what the girls would think of their mother having taken a lover.

She desperately wanted him to stay in England, but she realized he was a seaman at heart. Though forced into his profession, he had taken to it. The seas were home to him. It would be impossible for her to accompany him on his vessel. Not only would he be busy with all the varying responsibilities, but she needed to be here. She had the house party to host, where hopefully Lyric and Allegra might find a match. Mirella would make her come-out next spring, and Effie would follow in the one after that. Much as she wished she could leave England and sail with Drake around the world, her own obligations to her girls made that impractical.

Would she be willing to settle for a brief few days or weeks with Drake each time he sailed into port? He himself had said he could be gone as long as a year or two on sea voyages. His feelings for her might change during those long absences. Dinah knew hers would never change for him. If she were only able to snatch small pieces of him in the years to come, she would be willing to do so. She would live for those times and pray the loneliness in-between would not swallow her whole.

Drake moved to her side now, lacing his fingers through hers. Tears sprang to her eyes with the simple, romantic gesture. Everything between them had felt so very right from the beginning. It was unfair they had been placed in such an impossible situation. She knew, however, that attaining the position of captain had been his goal since he was a boy. She could not ask him to give up the sea. If he did, he might grow to resent her. No, she could never keep him from what he loved. She would have to settle for being his second love.

The sea would always be first in his heart.

"Are you excited to see your girls again?" Drake asked.

"I always am. I cannot tell you how hard it was waving goodbye to Pippa, knowing she would be gone for so long."

"From what you say, she has a bit of the adventurer in her."

"She does. Seth, being a former sea captain, will show her everything she has yearned to see. They love one another so much. It brings me such comfort knowing how well he will take care of her. I am ready for her to be home, though. Georgina, too."

"How long will she and Edgethorne honeymoon in Scotland?"

"They weren't really sure. They wed at Shadowcrest and then traveled the short distance to Edgefield, August's country estate in Surrey. He had never seen the property left to him by his mother, but he said she always spoke of Dalmara as being a magical place. They are so very much in love. I think they will stay the rest of the summer. I told them not to worry about being back in time for the house party."

He grinned. "Because it is a party to help your nieces find suitable husbands."

"Very much so."

"Why did they not make their come-outs as scheduled?"

Knowing they had the time, Dinah launched into the sordid story of her brother-in-law and nephew, and how they had wanted to hold Sophie for ransom when Adolphus lost his chance at becoming the next Duke of Seaton with James' return.

"Not only has their father ignored them from birth, but he also never contributed a farthing to their upbringing. When Allegra and Lyric learned just how expensive a come-out is and that James would be paying for everything, they balked at making their debuts into Polite Society."

He brushed his lips against her cheek. "They sound like very thoughtful young ladies."

"I consider them my own since they grew up alongside my four. I am the only mother they have ever known. I am grateful that they are allowing me to host the house party, though. It is an intimate affair, and you get to speak to people at length, getting to know them much better than during the Season."

Dinah explained a little about some of the rules of the *ton* and how after only a handful of dances, some ladies found themselves betrothed to men without even knowing their Christian names.

Drake shook his head. "I understand how arranged marriages are a part of life, but it's still hard to comprehend so many entering them, barely knowing one another."

"I did so," she reminded him. "I was a dutiful daughter. My father arranged the match, and I went along with it because I truly did not have a choice." She sighed. "I have told my girls they will never suffer in that manner. James, too, has assured them they can have as many Seasons as they wish. No one is pushing them from the safe confines of Shadowcrest. They will wed for love—or not at all."

He slipped his arm about her, drawing her to him. "You are a wonderful mother, Dinah. Though I have never thought of marrying myself, because I spend most of my life at sea, you make me wish I could have had children."

She wished she could have another babe. His babe. Everything she had learned about this man told her he would be an excellent father. Though she longed to approach him about this topic, even she knew it must never come to pass. She thought of the huge scandal which would play out, a widowed duchess having a child out of wedlock. It would ruin her—and her girls. They would suffer because of her indiscretion. Dinah could never allow it.

Even if her heart wished for a babe with Drake Andrews.

Sighing, she rested her head against his shoulder, living in the moment, not allowing herself to think of when they would be separated.

⇁⇉⇾⇽⇇↽

DRAKE SAVORED THE feel of Dinah next to him as the carriage turned and proceeded up the long lane that lead to Shadowcrest. He had come here once before, to bring Dinah back to James, who had been injured fighting a fire at his warehouse. He had briefly met the other members of the family before Dinah and he had set off for London.

Now, he would stay for a few days at his friend's country estate. He was eager to spend time with James and even his employer, the new Duchess of Seaton, beyond the business they would conduct. More than that, he was ready for more time alone with Dinah.

The Dowager Duchess of Seaton had proven to be the most remarkable woman of his acquaintance. Yes, he was physically attracted to her, but it was much more than that. He liked the person she was— clever, interesting, and extremely kind. Before getting to know her, he had thought all ladies of the *ton* to be the same, but Dinah Strong was a force to be reckoned with. His love for her had only grown stronger in the last few days in her company.

And Drake couldn't begin to think what his life would be like when they parted.

The carriage slowed, coming to a stop in front of the house. Glancing out the window, he saw a beaming James waiting to greet them. His friend was surrounded by four others, all Dinah's girls. Two were her daughters, and the other pair the twin nieces she had raised as her own. He did recall they all possessed what he now thought of as the Strong eyes, a cornflower blue. The nieces resembled one another, one having dark hair like Dinah's twins Pippa and Georgina, the other, hair a dark russet that showed its red in today's sunshine.

The other two daughters, though they had the Strong eyes, looked entirely different from the other women. He saw Lady Mirella, who was a few inches over five feet. Her auburn hair blazed different shades of red outdoors. Lady Euphemia, whom Dinah affectionately called Effie, was tall and lean, with the blond hair of Dinah's own mother.

James himself opened the carriage door, and Dinah gave him her hand. Drake followed close behind her, carrying the satchel Barnes had entrusted to him, watching as she was surrounded by her girls.

He turned to his oldest, dearest friend, and they embraced one another, slapping each other on the back.

"You are now wed to Mrs. Grant," he said, smiling at James. "And I hear congratulations are in order."

"Yes, Sophie will birth our firstborn come the end of September," James shared. "She and Aunt Matty are in the drawing room, awaiting the two of you."

By now, Dinah had joined them. "Come meet the girls again, Captain Andrews."

One by one, she introduced him again to her girls, who made their curtseys to him.

"Thank you for coming to visit James," Lady Effie said. "It gave Mama an excuse to come home and see us."

"I was happy to escort her here. Her Grace has talked about you—all of you—quite a bit to me. She has entertained me these past few days, ever since I returned to England."

He noted James cocked an eyebrow. Drake wanted to deflect any questions and held up the satchel he carried.

"I bear papers from Mr. Barnes at Neptune Shipping," he announced. "Reports that Her Grace is to review. Mr. Barnes knew I was coming for a visit and asked if I would deliver these to Her Grace, as well as give her details about my own voyage."

"Sophie will be delighted to talk business with you, Drake," James said. "But first, come in and let us chat a bit."

Dinah was swept away by the four young women, leaving him to enter the house with James.

"So, you have been keeping company with Dinah the past few days," his friend noted.

Not wanting to give away anything about their clandestine relationship, Drake said, "Her Grace has been more than kind to me."

"I recall when the two of you met. I'd never seen a man and woman flirt so in my entire life." James smiled. "And remember, I have seen you in action with women from all parts of the globe."

"Her Grace is a very attractive woman," he replied evenly.

"She is glowing, Drake," James pointed out as they followed the women up the stairs. "I have never seen her this way. And don't tell me it is because of some gentleman she has been seeing during the Season."

His friend knew him all too well. "There is an attraction between us," he began. "Her Grace is unique in every way."

James stopped on the landing of the stairs, staring at Drake. "What have the two of you been up to?"

"I have never been one to kiss and tell," he said brusquely. "But whatever we have done, we know nothing can come of it."

Drake started up the next flight of stairs, but James grasped his elbow, preventing any forward progress.

"Drake, you should not think like that."

He snorted, seeing the women were now out of sight. "What do you want me to say, James? I know my place. And I know Dinah's."

"Dinah, is it?"

"Yes," he spat out. "Dinah. The most extraordinary woman I have ever known."

"Biblically?" his friend teased.

"It is nothing to joke about, James," Drake chastised. "We are as unsuited as a couple might be. I am a child of the streets. She is a bloody duchess."

James took his elbow. "Let me say this. Dinah Strong is the most unpretentious woman you could meet, regardless of her position in Polite Society. If you want to be with her—and she wants the same—make it happen."

"I can't," he said, his throat thick with emotion. "Despite all that we have in common, we are still too different. She has more of her girls to launch into society. I would only be a hindrance." He met his friend's gaze. "Leave it be, James. We have enjoyed one another's company. We will continue to do so until I set sail again. Then it will be over and done."

He broke away, hurrying up the stairs, James catching up. They entered a large drawing room, with several groupings of seats running its entire length. He spied his employer, the former Mrs. Josiah Grant, along with another woman whom he recalled was James' aunt.

"Ah, Captain Andrews," the duchess said, extending her hand.

Drake took it and pressed her fingers lightly. He didn't feel quite right kissing her hand.

"It is good to see you again, Your Grace. I have brought documents and reports from Mr. Barnes for you to peruse."

Her eyes lit up at the talk of business. "Oh, I am glad to hear this, Captain. I always look forward to Mr. Barnes' visits. And we must spend time together so that you might tell me of your maiden voyage as captain of *Vesta*. I have sent for some tea. Let us enjoy a cup or two, and then we can adjourn to my study."

"I would be happy to meet with you, Your Grace."

The tea arrived, and Dinah assisted the Duchess of Seaton in pouring out since they were such a large group. An enjoyable hour passed, as the girls caught up their mother on news from the neighborhood and asked him questions about his most recent voyage, along with questions about his years with their brother. Drake noted they all referred to James as their brother and not half-brother. He wondered if it was something his friend had requested, or if Dinah had been responsible for bringing these siblings together.

For her part, Dinah told them of several events she had attended since she had last been at Shadowcrest for Lady Georgina's wedding to the Marquess of Edgethorne. Her stories were amusing and lighthearted. Never once did she mention any of her suitors.

James said, "While I know we have all enjoyed this time, I can tell my wife is champing at the bit to talk over business with Captain Andrews."

The duchess smiled fondly at her husband. "You know me all too well. Would you take Captain Andrews to my study, James? I will join him shortly."

He rose. "Thank you for having me. I look forward to your hospitality."

His friend led them from the drawing room and back downstairs, to a bright room filled with a large desk, several chairs, and a settee, as well as a globe of the world and shelves lined with books.

"Sophie has all manner of books here, as well as ledgers from the business. She can add and subtract more quickly in her head than I ever could writing the figures down in front of me. I hope you will have a good talk."

As James left the room, Drake opened the satchel and removed what lay within it. He set items in neat stacks so his employer would easily be able to locate documents as they spoke. Taking a seat in one of the chairs in front of the desk, he wondered where his bedchamber was—and how far away it was from Dinah's. He looked forward to bedding her in an actual bed, though they had been rather creative in finding places to make love this week.

The duchess entered, and he sprang to his feet.

"No need to be so formal, Captain," she said cheerfully. "Thank you for your patience. I find I am in need of a chamber pot at least once an hour. The doctor told me it is because the baby presses against my bladder."

"I see," he said, a bit taken aback at her frankness, but charmed by her, nonetheless. Drake could see why James had been drawn to her.

She took a seat, glancing at the documents laid out on her desk, nodding to herself.

Then she met his gaze. "We will certainly talk business during this time together, Captain, but I have one question for you."

"I am happy to answer anything, Your Grace. You favored me by making me captain of *Vesta*. I owe you more than I can ever repay."

She smiled at him. "What I would like to know is how long you and Dinah have been in love with one another."

CHAPTER EIGHT

D RAKE SPUTTERED. "WHAT?"

"Oh, come now, Captain," the duchess chided. "I may appear slow as I lumber about with this protruding belly, but I am far from slow mentally. I see what is before me. Dinah is radiating joy. While I have always found her to be a happy, pleasant woman, the widow who turned up at Shadowcrest today is different from the woman I have come to know."

He let out a long breath. "Is it that obvious?"

"To me. And Aunt Matty. Our eyes met a time or two as one or the other of you spoke. We both saw the surreptitious glances you gave one another when you thought no one else was looking your way."

He winced, knowing he had looked admiringly—and longingly—at Dinah during their time in the drawing room.

"Do you think her girls noticed?"

"If anyone did, it would be Mirella. She is especially close to her mother and having almost made her come-out, much more aware of the relationships between men and women. You were not obvious, Captain. Just a bit careless a time or two. Dinah, as well."

"I apologize, Your Grace."

She looked puzzled. "For what?"

Drake couldn't say.

"Listen to me carefully, Captain Andrews," the duchess said. "I am quite an admirer of Dinah. She has done an outstanding job raising that bevy of girls, with no help from her husband or brother-in-law. All six of them are polite, kind, and gracious. Dinah has also promised them they will never find themselves in the circumstances she did, marrying a man she barely knew and could never love. But it is time she found some happiness herself, especially since Georgie and Pippa have been shining examples of women who have found love."

"I did not say I loved her," he said defensively.

The duchess' eyes narrowed. "Are you telling me you do not?" she demanded.

He raked a hand through his hair. "All right. I do. Love her, that is. But it would be impossible for us to be together, Your Grace."

She sniffed. "You are telling *me* of the impossible, Captain Andrews? I was a woman scorned by the *ton*. My father wed me to Josiah Strong at a young age, officially ostracizing me from Polite Society. My husband was wealthy as Midas, but he had worked hard to establish his shipping line and build a business empire. Gentlemen of the *ton* do not work. They inherit their wealth and then never discuss it. I went from girlish daydreams of thinking I would find a handsome husband in Polite Society to being an instant outcast upon my marriage."

She leaned forward in her chair, resting folded hands on her desk. "But I had something women of the *ton* did not. An interesting life. A husband who treated me as an equal. Josiah taught me everything about business that he had learned over decades of experience. I soaked up everything I could and then began running Neptune Shipping before his death. I inherited the company upon his passing. That only made me even more of a pariah in Polite Society."

The duchess smiled. "And yet I managed to wed a duke. Yes, there was a smattering of gossip about us when the Season began, but we became friendly with a good deal of others and made several influential friends amongst those in the *ton*. It would not have mattered, though, because we love one another a great deal. If it had only been the two of us against the world, we would have accepted that."

Drake shook his head. "Your story is different from ours, Your Grace. First, James is a duke. Even he has told me dukes are a law unto themselves. And you were a wealthy widow. In marrying my friend, you had not only his protection, but that of his name. His ducal title. *His* wealth, as well as that of your own."

She frowned. "Go on."

"I have no title. No wealth. Yes, my recent increase in pay, thanks to my new position as captain of *Vesta*, certainly has me more comfortable than in the past, but I could not afford to buy even a small house on that salary. The most I could do is take a few rooms in an unfashionable part of town. Dinah would lose her own title and position in society if we wed. She would no longer be a part of the world she has inhabited since birth."

Smiling, the duchess told him, "The way she looked at you, I do not think that would matter to her."

"But it matters to me!" he said, slamming his hand on her desk. "I cannot take her from all she has known. Sentence her to a life of exile from her peers. Worse, she has only married off two of her girls. She has four more to take in hand and launch into Polite Society. How do you think her daughters and nieces might fare with their mother wed to a sea captain, a man who is home only a couple of weeks at most before he sets off on a voyage that would take me from her for a year or two?"

Frustrated, he stood and began pacing the room. "I would leave her to a life away from all she has known as I earned my living. Why, she would not even have enough coin to hire help to cook or clean. And the girls would become laughingstocks, subject to ridicule, their chances of making a good match gone."

He stopped in his tracks. "Yes, I love her. Yes, she loves me. But there are more than the two of us to consider. Even after her four girls wed, I can't see how I could remove Dinah from all she has known."

Drake fell into the chair again. "I won't do it to her. I can't make her miserable."

With sympathy in her eyes, the duchess said, "But you will both be miserable apart."

He nodded. "We have resigned ourselves to that fate. I wanted to walk away before we became too involved. Dinah convinced me to stay. To enjoy what little time we had together."

"I could keep you in port," she offered. "Not send you out for several weeks. Even months."

"No. I would not wish for you to show me such favoritism, much less keep my crew from working and earning their own livings." He sighed. "Dinah and I know we have no future together. We are simply living in the moment now, savoring the time we have together. I have told her that she deserves happiness and should wed again. By the time I return to England after *Vesta's* next voyage, I fully expect she will have married again."

He raked both hands through his hair. "Enough of this talk, Your Grace. Shall we get down to the business at hand? Mr. Barnes prepared a report regarding the goods I traded and those I brought back. I would like to tell you about my first time at sea, being a captain." He paused. "It was a very lucrative trip, Your Grace."

She looked upon him, sadness in her eyes. "Please go ahead, Captain. Tell me everything. I am eager to hear about your journey."

⤜⤜⤜⤛⤛⤛

WHILE DRAKE WAS closeted with Sophie, Dinah focused totally on her girls.

Mirella had recovered nicely from the broken elbow she had suffered earlier in the spring, thrilled the plaster had finally been removed

80

from her arm. She told Dinah she had been practicing her pianoforte more than ever, trying to make up for the lost time at the instrument. Effie had been riding quite a bit, and she had also found homes for two of the strays she had taken in. Her daughter had a tender heart where animals were concerned.

The most time was spent discussing the upcoming house party, with Dinah wanting input from her two nieces, reminding them this was their debut into Polite Society and that it would be a small group present at Shadowcrest, allowing them to get to know others in a cozy atmosphere. She described various activities she had already planned to take place, and they went over menu ideas. She told the twins the three of them would meet with Cook and Miss Forrester tomorrow morning to discuss in detail the food which would be served.

What Allegra and Lyric did not know was that Dinah had already spoken to Madame Dumas regarding new gowns for the house party. The modiste had made up some new clothes for her nieces back in the spring before the twins had come to her, saying they no longer wished to make their come-outs with Georgina and Mirella.

Since she already had current measurements, Madame and her seamstresses were already hard at work, sewing several new gowns for each twin to wear at the house party given in their honor. Dinah would bring these back with her when the Season ended and she left town to return to the country for the rest of the year.

She wondered when Drake would be leaving England again. Part of her wanted to go to Sophie, begging her not to send him away too soon, but she could never do that. Drake was a proud man, living out his dream now by captaining his own ship. She would not be selfish and keep him and his crew in port.

Drake and Sophie rejoined them for tea, Drake taking a chair opposite her. Dinah did her best not to look at him, but she found it almost impossible to keep from doing so. He was simply the best-looking man she had ever come upon. It was hard to believe that she had made love with him several times in the past few days. She wondered what room Sophie had placed Drake in, because she definitely planned to couple with him in a bed after the household went to sleep for the night.

They had a lively dinner together, with her nephew Caleb, the Shadowcrest steward, and Miss Feathers, Effie's governess, also joining them. The girls continued to ask Drake about his travels with James.

"If you would like to go riding tomorrow, Captain Andrews," Effie offered, "I would be happy to show you about Shadowcrest."

Drake laughed. "I have never been atop a horse, Lady Effie. I am never on land long enough to learn how to ride."

Effie waved a hand dismissively. "You say that, Captain Andrews, yet I taught James to ride in about a week's time. He took to it well. I wager you would do the same."

James spoke up. "If you do want to learn to ride, Drake, Effie is the one to teach you. She has the patience of Job and a way with horses. With all animals, in fact."

"I only will be here tomorrow and possibly the day after. I know Her Grace has prior engagements she has committed to in town, so I must see her returned."

Dinah had suspended those very engagements, but she supposed Drake wished to return to town and his crew. She wondered if he and Sophie had decided upon the date for *Vesta* to sail again, deciding she really didn't wish to learn it. Knowing the deadline when he would leave London would only add to her heartache.

After dinner, they retired to the drawing room so that Mirella could play for them. Mirella called James to the piano and encouraged Drake to join him. The two men did, and her daughter began playing a lively tune, one which James and Drake immediately began to sing along to. It was quite bawdy in nature, causing them all to laugh aloud. Dinah thought Drake's singing voice a wonderful one, recalling how she used to play for her own sweetheart, and how his singing hurt her ears.

When the piece ended, Dinah asked her daughter, "Where did you learn such a song?"

Mirella grinned shamelessly. "James sang it to me a few times, and I was able to add chords to the tune. Captain Andrews, you sing quite well, even better than James does."

"You should see him dance," James said. "Sailors often have contests on deck, where a fiddle is produced and sometimes a pipe. No one can compete with Drake here. He dances the best jig of any seafaring man."

She longed to teach Drake the waltz, thinking he would take to it as well as he did everything else, but their time to part drew near. There would not be enough hours in the day to teach him the dance, much less have him accompany her and dance it at a *ton* ball.

Dinah yawned deliberately. "Oh, I must be more tired than I realized. It is the carriage ride from town to Kent, I suppose. It is not that long, but traveling always seems to make me weary."

She turned to Drake. "Has Miss Forrester shown you which is your bedchamber yet?"

"No," he replied. "I am not certain where I am sleeping tonight."

Only Dinah knew what he referred to, and she coughed to keep from smiling.

Lyric spoke up. "Miss Forrester put Captain Andrews in Georgie and Pippa's old room. The twins always shared a room, as Allegra and I do."

"And Effie and I have always shared, too," Mirella told Drake.

Dinah was pleased to hear the news of his location, for it was next to her own bedchamber. She had kept her rooms after Seaton's death, but when James wed Sophie, Dinah vacated the duchess' rooms and moved down the hall to a new bedchamber.

Drake yawned. "I suppose I am tired myself."

"Then let me take you upstairs, Captain," Dinah offered. "I can show you to your bedchamber."

They said goodnight to the others, but everyone else also decided to turn in. James remarked how country hours were different from those in town and that they usually went to bed early and rose early.

The entire group followed Dinah and Drake down the corridor to the west wing. Dinah stopped at her own twins' former room, thinking of her girls being loved and happy as wives.

"This is where your things will be, Captain Andrews," she said. "I am sure Miss Forrester has provided everything for you, but if you have need of anything else, I am the next door down from you, the one we just passed. Feel free to seek me out if something is missing that you require."

"Goodnight, Your Grace. Goodnight to all," Drake called, and then he entered the bedchamber, closing the door.

For her part, Dinah went to her room as the others did the same. Only Mirella followed Dinah.

"I noticed you did not bring your lady's maid with you, Mama."

"I knew I would only be at Shadowcrest for a couple of days, so I left her in town. I will ring for Miss Forrester. She can help me to undress."

"Let me help you, Mama," her daughter offered.

"Why, that would be lovely, Mirella."

"I can do much more now that I have two arms to work with," Mirella teased, following Dinah inside the bedchamber.

She had only brought a small valise with her since she had so many gowns already at Shadowcrest. Miss Forrester had already unpacked it, placing her night rail and dressing gown across the bed and her brush and comb on the dressing table.

Mirella helped her to undress and into her clothing for bed. Dinah bit back a smile, knowing everything would soon be removed again by Drake.

"Shall I brush out your hair for you, Mama?"

"Yes, my darling. You have always enjoyed doing so. It does soothe me."

She sat at the dressing table, Mirella removing the pins and placing them in a bowl on the table before brushing Dinah's hair until it shone.

"Would you like me to plait it for you?"

"No. I may do so later. I think I will read a bit until I grow sleepy."

Mirella sat down the brush and said, "Captain Andrews is quite an interesting man."

"Yes," Dinah said carefully, knowing how astute Mirella could be. She hoped her daughter had not picked up on anything between them.

"You seem to be comfortable with one another."

She would not lie to her girl and decided to be as open as she could. "Yes, I have felt an affinity with him from the first time James introduced us. I do believe we formed a special bond when he came to Shadowcrest last year and brought me to town to tend to James after the warehouse fire."

Mirella's gaze met hers. "I like him quite a bit, Mama. I think he likes you, too."

"We have spent time in one another's company these past few days while he was waiting for Mr. Barnes to finish up his reports so that Captain Andrews could bring them here to Sophie at Shadowcrest. The captain is very kind and intelligent. I have enjoyed being with him."

Her daughter reached for her mother's hand and squeezed it. "I know Georgie said you have had many suitors this Season, Mama, but you have yet to speak of a single one of them. Do any of them interest you the way Captain Andrews does?"

Her throat tightened. "No," she admitted. "I had thought it a possibility to wed again, Mirella, but I am not looking to be in a similar situation to what I was before. After seeing your two sisters wed for love, I believe that would be the only reason I would consider a second marriage. Since no gentleman of the *ton* has caught my fancy, I will remain a widow and your mother."

She smoothed Mirella's hair. "Do not worry about me, dearest. Helping you find a good match will be my priority next spring when you make your come-out."

"I do not want you to sacrifice your own happiness for me, Mama."

"I won't. But you—all my girls—are what bring me the most joy in life. I long to see each of you happily wed in the next few years."

"I think it was a good thing that I did not make my come-out this year, Mama," Mirella reflected. "It gave me more time to be with those I love, here at Shadowcrest. I know once I wed, this will no longer be my home."

Dinah cradled her daughter's cheeks. "Shadowcrest will always be your home. Yes, your loyalties will lie with your husband and the new family the two of you create, but you will always have a place here."

Mirella kissed Dinah's cheek. "I am glad you came home, Mama, if only for a couple of days. Goodnight."

"Goodnight, my love."

She watched her daughter exit the room and went to the chair by the window. Sitting in it, she bided her time. It would be best if Drake spent the night in her bed since his bedchamber was next to Lyric and Allegra's and across from Mirella and Effie's. She would have to watch herself tonight and tamp down some of the enthusiastic noises she had a tendency to make while Drake made love to her.

After half an hour passed, she rose, intending to go and retrieve Drake. When she opened her door, however, he stood before her, his hand raised, ready to rap on it.

Quickly, she pulled him inside, closing and locking the door. They fell into one another's arms, kissing hungrily for several minutes.

Then Drake swept her off her feet and carried her to the bed, placing her gently upon it.

His eyes darkened with desire as he gazed down at her. He smiled. "It will be interesting to finally bed you *in* a bed, Duchess."

CHAPTER NINE

D INAH COULDN'T HELP but laugh. "Oh, come here, you," she said, claiming his hand and pulling him down to her.

Drake fell onto the bed, the two of them giggling as if they were five-year-olds up to mischief.

He turned her so they faced one another, his hand cupping her buttocks. "Do you think you can be quiet tonight, love? I thought the staff, led by Powell, would race into the conservatory the other day."

She sniffed haughtily. "I can be as quiet as a church mouse, Captain." Then another fit of giggles hit her.

Drake silenced them by kissing her. Oh, how this man could kiss! He tended to her mouth before moving on to other places on her. He had told her at the beginning of their love affair just how powerful a kiss could be. After being kissed by him hundreds of times in areas she had no idea could be kissed, she now understood his words.

For her part, Dinah responded to each kiss, savoring his taste and scent, her fingers dancing along his magnificent body, hardened by hard labor over his many years at sea. She took the initiative now, undressing him first, kissing her way up and down his frame with every piece she removed. Drake returned the favor, ridding Dinah of her clothing, his lips caressing her everywhere.

For a moment, she contemplated what life without him would be like, their time drawing to an end. Shaking the thought off, she kissed him with everything she had. His large hands stroked her back as they kissed, making her feel cherished.

When it came time to come together, he turned on his back, capturing her waist and lifting her high, impaling her on his cock. As she took it inside her, a surge of power rushed through her.

"Move and see what feels good to the both of us," he told her.

Dinah did as he instructed, finding her way in a new position, learning what pleased her and Drake. She found her rhythm, and the intensity between them increased, exploding in an earthshattering orgasm for her. For his part, Drake lifted her off him and rolled, spending in the chamber pot next to the bed.

He climbed back into bed with her, cradling her in his arms, tenderly kissing her nape as his palms caressed her belly and breasts.

"Go to sleep," he whispered in her ear. "For the first time, I can stay with you."

"Not all night," she murmured sleepily. "You must be gone by dawn."

He pressed his warm lips against her shoulder. "I will."

When Dinah next awoke, it was to Drake's kiss. He made love to her again, this time slowly and tenderly, before once again sending his seed into the chamber pot. Afterward, he rose from the bed and dressed quickly.

"I will go and trade my chamber pot for yours," he told her. "I don't wish to leave any proof that I was in your bed."

She knew he had because she caught the scent of him on one of the pillows. She would say nothing of it, though.

He left the room and returned less than a minute later, exchanging his chamber pot for hers.

"The maid will understand my seed being in mine."

"Do all men pleasure themselves if alone?" she asked, curious.

"Most, I assume. Sailors at sea definitely do, especially when they are at sea for many weeks." He grinned. "And I am a sailor, first and foremost, even if I am a captain now."

Leaning down, he pressed a soft kiss upon her lips. "I love you. I will see you at breakfast."

Before she could reply, he was gone.

Dinah fell back asleep and awoke a short time later. Being in the country, she always seemed to be up with daylight.

When she went downstairs and joined the others in the breakfast room, Drake gave her a wink.

"I'd like to show you some of Shadowcrest today," James said to his friend. "Not on horseback, of course."

"You could see more if you learned to ride a horse," Effie said, causing Drake to laugh.

"Perhaps the next time I am in England, you might take me in hand, my lady, and teach me the finer points of riding."

Effie stroked the cat sitting in her lap. "I would be happy to do so. When will you next sail, Captain Andrews? And return?"

Dinah's heart stilled at the question.

"That is something Her Grace and I will be deciding later today," Drake said.

She released the breath she had held, not even realizing she did so. Of course, it would be Sophie who would map out the next voyage Drake would undertake with his crew.

"I plan to seek Captain Andrews' advice on a good number of things today," Sophie said. "With his decades of experience at sea, he has valuable information to share."

"You had him for a couple of hours yesterday," James pointed out. "At least let me visit with him this morning."

"Ah, being fought over by a duke and duchess," Drake noted. "Who would have thought that might happen to me?"

Those at the table laughed heartily.

"When are we meeting with Cook and Miss Forrester, Aunt Dinah?" Allegra asked. "I have had a few ideas about the menus to be served."

"I have, too," Lyric exclaimed. "And I will admit I am a bit curious about the guest list, as well."

"We can meet after breakfast and discuss your ideas then," she told the twins.

Sophie went to her office to get some work done, and James and Drake excused themselves, leaving to walk parts of Shadowcrest. Effie decided to join them, even if they were walking and not riding. Mirella went off to practice her pianoforte, while Lyric and Allegra accompanied Dinah to the kitchens. They sat with Cook and Miss Forrester, discussing various dishes to be served, especially the desserts.

"If you would like, Cook, I can bring back a few scullery maids from town with me to help with the party."

The older woman breathed a sigh of relief. "That would be appreciated, Your Grace. This is a large house party you are talking about. The more hands, the merrier."

They drew up a meal plan for each day of the house party, including a few outdoor teas to be held, both on the terrace and by the lake.

"This is not our final menu," Dinah cautioned, "but I believe we have made good headway this morning."

"Then I am going for a walk," Allegra declared. "Would you like to come along, Aunt Dinah?"

"I think I will stay here. I am hoping to lure Sophie away from her work."

"You should," Lyric said. "She is always working. I keep telling her when the babe comes, she will have to count upon Mr. Barnes to shoulder more of the load."

Dinah left the kitchens and made her way to the room dedicated as Sophie's office. She tapped lightly on the door and entered, seeing Sophie deep into thought as she held a paper in her hand.

"Is it that complicated?" she asked.

Sophie chuckled. "Business has a tendency to be complicated at times." She paused. "Not to Captain Andrews, however."

She frowned. "What do you mean? He does not have a background in business."

"He doesn't—and yet his instincts are quite good. With his sailing experience, he shared countless insights with me yesterday. It is almost a shame to waste him at sea, because I certainly could use him in the shipping and warehouse offices."

Her heart skipped a beat. "Would you make that kind of offer to him?"

"I very well might, Dinah." Sophie paused, gazing at her intently. "And not merely because the two of you are in love."

"Oh!" she exclaimed, leaping to her feet. Conscious she had done so, she took a seat again. "What did you say?"

"It is obvious to me," Sophie said. "I noticed the bond between the two of you right away. It was the first thing I asked Captain Andrews about once we were behind closed doors."

Dinah felt her face flushing with heat. "Thank you for not saying anything in front of the girls."

"*Do* you love him, Dinah?" Sophie pressed.

She nodded. "Yes. Very much so. But we are in a unique situation, Sophie. He has finally risen to be the captain of a Neptune Ship, something he aimed for his entire life. The sea is in his blood. I cannot take him from that."

Pausing, she then added, "He is a most proud man. If he left his ship in order to accept a new position with your company, he would be miserable. He might want to do so now because he loves me, but in the long run? I fear he would resent me. Because of that, I cannot ask him to stay, nor would I ask you to keep him in port longer than he should be. There is also his crew to consider. Drake would not want them kept from their livelihood."

"Will you wait for him? Try and see him between voyages?"

"I hope to," she said. "I am not confident that he would agree to such a plan, though. Drake believes I should wed again. A man from my world."

She burst into tears. "Oh, Sophie, I am so frustrated by the entire situation."

Sophie came to her, embracing her. "I know how much I love James. If we could not be together, I haven't a clue what I would do."

"We know the time is coming when we must part. I have tried my best to prepare myself for it, but I fear misery will engulf me. Yet I would not trade a minute of the time we have had together. It has been so very precious."

She wiped away her tears with the back of her hand. "I am grateful for what Drake has shown me. I had never known love before. While my heart will break when he sails away, it was the right thing to do. To be together while we could."

A knock sounded at the door. Before Sophie could call out for the servant to enter, Forrester hurried into the room, his brow furrowed. He bore a silver tray in hand, a letter atop it.

"Your Grace, this just came for you. The messenger is getting something to eat in the kitchens and can return with a reply if you wish."

It was obvious to Dinah that the butler had spoken to this messenger and already had a good idea of the contents within the letter.

"Thank you, Forrester," Sophie said, dismissing him.

Forrester left the room, closing the door. Dinah looked to Sophie.

"With Forrester looking so grim, I am almost afraid to break the seal," her friend admitted.

"If it is bad news, perhaps I should read it first," she offered. "You must think of the babe."

Handing the letter over, Sophie said, "Yes, go ahead."

With trepidation, Dinah broke the seal, opening the letter. She read it, shock filling her.

Raising her eyes, she met Sophie's gaze. "It is Mr. Barnes," she revealed. "He has suffered a heart attack." Dinah paused. "He is not expected to live."

CHAPTER TEN

DRAKE RETURNED TO the house with James, having seen as much of Shadowcrest as they could on foot. Their last stop was the stables, where James showed off the horse he had learned to ride on. Lady Effie told Drake about several of the mounts in the stable, even indicating which one she thought would be best for *him* to learn to ride upon.

"I will keep that in mind, my lady," he said, laughing. "For my next visit."

They left Effie in the stables, visiting a mother cat and her latest litter of kittens. As they entered the foyer, Forrester met them, a pained expression upon his face.

"Your Grace, Her Grace is making plans to return to town immediately."

"What?" James roared. "It is not safe for her to do so. The babe will be here in two months' time." Determination filled his face. "This will not happen."

Drake knew that his friend was upset, worried for the health and safety of both mother and child. The duchess would not be planning something of this nature, however, unless the unthinkable had happened.

Something was wrong with her other babe—Neptune Shipping.

"Do you know what prompted this sudden decision, Forrester?"

James asked the butler.

"A messenger arrived with a note for Her Grace. It seems that Mr. Barnes is gravely ill."

"No wonder she thinks to go to London," James said, shaking his head. "I will go in her place and take care of whatever she needs done."

The butler left them, and Drake touched his friend's arm. "Your wife is determined to do this, James. You have to realize that Mr. Barnes is as family to her. While I know she loves you a great deal, you must consider that it hasn't been that long since she lost Mr. Grant. He was both father figure and mentor to her. Losing Mr. Barnes now must have her frantic with worry. Not only for him—but for the business she runs."

James raked both hands through his hair. "You are right, Drake. I probably shouldn't try and stop her."

"Then make the journey as easy as you can on her," he recommended.

"I will go and speak to Sophie now. Will you and Dinah accompany us?"

"Of course. Anything you wish."

He went to his bedchamber, packing the few items he had brought, and took the valise to Dinah's door, knocking upon her door. She opened it, her own valise in hand.

"Oh, I thought you were one of the footmen coming to collect this."

"I have heard Mr. Barnes is ill. James has asked that we return to London with them."

He took the valise from her, and she followed him from the room.

As they made their way downstairs, she told him, "It was a heart attack. The note was sent by Mr. Samuel, whom I gather is a valued employee at Sophie's company."

"Yes, Samuel serves as secretary to Her Grace and Mr. Barnes. He knows quite a bit about the business."

He set down their luggage in the foyer. "James is upset about his wife making such a journey in her delicate condition."

"I know how much Sophie already loves this babe," Dinah said. "She would do nothing to risk it."

Glancing up, he saw James escorting his wife down the stairs. Sophie's hand protectively guarded her burgeoning belly.

When they reached the bottom, she said, "Thank you for agreeing to come with us. I am quite concerned about Mr. Barnes."

James cleared his throat. "We have discussed it. Usually, the journey from here to town takes between two-and-a-half and three hours. The horses will be walking the entire way, however, so as not to jar the carriage—and Sophie—overly much. It will take much longer to reach our destination, but it is the safest way to travel such a distance."

Lady Mirella came hurrying down the stairs. "Is it true? You are leaving?"

Dinah explained what had happened to Mr. Barnes and that they would be departing immediately.

Her daughter embraced her. "Please write to us, Mama. Let us know how Mr. Barnes fares."

Forrester appeared, announcing that the carriage awaited them. As the group moved to go outside, Drake felt something touch his sleeve and turned, seeing Lady Mirella there. He paused.

"Take care of Mama, Captain Andrews," she said. "And yourself."

"I will, my lady," he promised.

She hesitated a moment. "If you truly love Mama—and she loves you—then marry her. She deserves a bit of happiness after a lifetime of doing for others."

Shock ran through him, and Drake started to protest, but the young woman cut him off.

"The others may not have noticed, but I did. Mama is happier than I have ever seen her, and it is all because of you, Captain."

He swallowed painfully. "We do have feelings for one another, my lady, but I'm afraid we can never act upon them."

Anger sparked in her eyes. "Why not?" she demanded.

"Because neither your mother nor I would wish to ruin your chances of making a suitable match, much less that of your sister and cousins. Marriage between us would inevitably bring that about."

Mirella shook her head vehemently. "And I say to you, Captain Andrews, to follow your heart. That is what I plan to do, as well as Effie and my cousins. Mama has told us to wed only for love. None of us would consider marriage to a man who looked down upon the match Mama herself had made. If he did, then he would not be the man for any of us. Keep that in mind, Captain, and take care of her."

Lady Mirella released his arm and turned away, heading back up the stairs.

Drake joined the others, the last to enter the carriage. He was shaken by what Mirella Strong had said to him.

Could there be a future for him and Dinah?

Her fingers sought his, and he threaded them together, comforted by her touch.

They arrived in London seven hours later, having stopped to change out the horses at one point. Though obviously fatigued after so many hours of travel, the duchess demanded they go straight to Mr. Barnes' residence first. The coachman took them to a small house several blocks north of the London docks. They all climbed from the carriage, James striding toward the door and knocking upon it.

A servant answered, and James said, "It is the Duke and Duchess of Seaton who have come to see how Mr. Barnes is."

The maid admitted them, asking them to wait in a small parlor, which was opposite an even smaller dining room. The women took a seat, while the men remained on their feet.

Minutes later, an older woman in her late fifties or early sixties entered the room. Her resemblance to Mr. Barnes was obvious.

She curtseyed to them, saying, "I am Miss Barnes, sister to Mr. Barnes. I keep his house for him. I assume you are here to see how my brother is doing."

The duchess rose, taking Miss Barnes' hands in her own. "We are. Please, tell us how he is."

"It was a heart attack," Miss Barnes confirmed. "My brother is in very poor condition, Your Grace. The doctor does not believe he has long to live."

A cry of distress came from the duchess, and James went to his wife, guiding her to a seat.

"I am so very sorry to hear this, Miss Barnes," the duchess said. "Mr. Barnes has been with Neptune Shipping a great many years. I value him not only as my best employee, but he is my good friend."

Miss Barnes smiled. "He is most fond of you, Your Grace. From the start, he was filled with nothing but admiration for you. He is always praising how astute you are in business matters."

"Is it possible for me to see him?" the duchess asked.

"You may if you wish, but he might not know you are there," Miss Barnes said.

"I will accompany you," James said firmly, taking his wife by the elbow and helping her to rise. The three left the room.

That left Drake with Dinah, and he went to sit beside her, slipping an arm about her shoulders.

"This is terrible news," she said. "Sophie already works so hard in running Neptune Shipping. If she loses Mr. Barnes, I do not know what she will do."

"There is always the possibility that Mr. Samuel could step in," he said, not knowing enough about the secretary, but trying to give Dinah some hope.

They sat together, no words necessary, until James and Sophie entered the room again. Drake noticed Miss Barnes was no longer with them.

Tears streamed down the duchess' face as she told them, "He is gone. He was conscious at the end. We got to say our goodbyes to one another. I was able to tell him how much he meant to me, both as an employee and friend." Her voice broke, and James slipped an arm about her waist.

"We should go, my love," James said quietly. "You are exhausted, physically and emotionally."

James asked Drake to see the women to the carriage, and he left the room again. Knowing his friend, James was likely not only comforting Miss Barnes, but assuring the woman that he would see to the funeral expenses.

James joined them in the carriage, confirming Drake's suspicions.

"I told Miss Barnes we will handle all costs regarding Mr. Barnes' funeral."

"Thank you," the duchess whispered, her fingers seeking those of her husband.

"Miss Barnes will let us know when the funeral will be held. She thought tomorrow would be too soon, but she hoped to hold the service the following day."

They reached the ducal townhouse, and Drake went inside with them, not wanting to leave Dinah just yet. James told Powell to send a tray up for him and the duchess and see that Dinah and Drake were also fed.

Before the duke and duchess went upstairs, she looked to Drake. "Will you come and see me tomorrow morning, Captain?"

"Of course, Your Grace," he replied, thinking she might want to make him a liaison between her and the shipping offices for the next few days.

He went with Dinah to the winter parlor, where Powell had laid out a cold supper of ham, cheese, and bread for them. Drake pressed a glass of wine into Dinah's trembling hands.

"Drink this. We both need it after such a hellish day."

She took a sip and set down the glass. "I am terribly worried about Sophie," she admitted.

"This will be hard on her, losing such a valued man as Mr. Barnes," he agreed.

She met his gaze. "You must help her in any way you can, Drake. She will need to depend upon others to get through this time. She told me how much she had enjoyed your conversation yesterday. How much knowledge you possess."

"I will do whatever I can to help Her Grace through this difficult time," he promised.

They ate, neither one of them consuming much, and he told her to go to bed and get some rest. Drake took Dinah in his arms, kissing her softly, telling her it had been a long day.

"I am glad you will be back tomorrow morning," she said.

"I will do whatever is asked of me."

He kissed her again and told her goodnight. Leaving, he retired once more to *Vesta*, hating that he must spend the nights away from her after they had coupled. He stripped off his clothes and lay sleeplessly in his bunk for a long while, contemplating what Mr. Barnes' death would mean for Neptune Shipping.

And what Lady Mirella had said to him.

CHAPTER ELEVEN

THE NEXT MORNING, Drake returned to his friend's townhouse and was immediately shown into a room he had yet to see. The duchess sat behind a large desk, papers scattered across it. Seated before her was Mr. Samuel, who flipped through pages of some document, a frown on his face.

"Captain Andrews," Powell announced.

"Ah, yes, come in, Captain," Her Grace said, motioning for Drake to come closer.

"Good morning, Your Grace. Mr. Samuel."

The secretary nodded brusquely, returning to the pages he held.

"Please sit," the duchess told Drake. "Give me a moment."

He took the other seat in front of the desk, his eyes perusing the array of papers on the desk as the duchess fingered through them.

"Here it is, Mr. Samuel." She passed a page to the secretary.

Taking it, he skimmed it, nodding to himself. "Yes. This confirms it." Samuel stood. "I will take care of the matter at once, Your Grace."

"Thank you, Mr. Samuel. And I will let you and the others at the shipping offices and warehouse know about the arrangements for Mr. Barnes as soon as we hear from his sister later today. Naturally, all workers will be given the time off to attend the funeral."

"I will tell the others, Your Grace. Good day."

The secretary left, and the duchess turned her attention to Drake.

"Thank you for coming, Captain Andrews." She folded her hands, placing them in her lap. "If you do not mind, I would like to continue our conversation from yesterday."

They had been speaking of tasks each sailor performed on a ship, and Drake picked up where they had left off. Following that discussion, Her Grace asked numerous questions of him. They discussed numerous trade routes, how the calendar and weather affected those routes, and what supplies were traded in various ports around the world. She referred back to his captain's log, which she had open on her desk, along with the report Mr. Barnes had prepared regarding the cargo brought back by *Vesta* on its latest run. The duchess was very interested in how he was able to return with more Merino wool and whale oil than had been anticipated.

"It was in the negotiations, Your Grace," he told her. "As you know, each captain is given a certain amount of leeway when bringing in goods for trade and taking items native to a country in those trades."

"But you returned with far more than the usual, Captain," she pointed out. "I want to know how."

He shrugged. "I would say it was a number of things."

"Your charm?" she asked, smiling.

"Possibly. I will say that over the years, I have become quite familiar with various customs common in the different countries my vessels have visited. I believe knowing about these customs—and acknowledging them—puts my hosts in a better overall mood as we work to hammer out trade agreements."

"All captains should be doing this," she insisted. She thought a moment. "Walk me through a negotiation. Pretend that I have whale oil which you desire, and you have British goods that I want. How would we begin?"

Drake said, "I will need to leave the room and enter again."

He saw curiosity on her face as he rose and exited, immediately returning again. He greeted her with a few words she did not understand, smiling as he did so. Drake switched to a different native tongue and once more greeted her, seeing her bafflement.

"The first thing I did in my negotiations was make certain I greeted whomever I planned to do business with in their native tongue, even if the negotiator was British or European. Recognizing the language of various islands we call upon sets a certain tone. During my years at sea, I have picked up a smattering of several languages. When *Vesta* called at Fiji or Samoa or Tonga, I made certain I used what I knew to put others at ease."

"That is a gift, Captain Andrews," the duchess declared. "And a brilliant way to begin a business negotiation."

"I did that throughout the Polynesian Triangle."

She frowned. "I am not familiar with that term."

"It is merely a region in the Pacific Ocean which is anchored at three points by three different island groups at each of those corners. Hawai'i. Easter Island. And New Zealand. What lies within the triangle shape formed are the islands consisting of Polynesia."

"And you know a bit about each of the islands?" she pressed.

"The ones we call at. A few of the others, which I visited on various voyages over the years, ones which Neptune Shipping ships may or may not call upon. Frankly, though, there are hundreds, if not thousands, of others."

The duchess retrieved an atlas, turning to a section which had maps of the area. They talked for length about which islands her vessels went to and the goods those islands traded in return. She asked him about those island groups which her company did not have a business relationship with, and Drake talked at length, telling her as much as he could.

"This is all fascinating information, Captain. It makes me want to expand my fleet and trade with places we have never gone before. Of course, that would mean building more ships and redrawing trade routes. Consolidating some and expanding others." She sighed. "We are already in the midst of building a new ship. It would take much time and thought to decide of others to be built."

"If you ever wish for suggestions regarding a new ship, Your Grace, I would be happy to give you a few ideas. Having spent most of my life aboard them, I have come to see many benefits and yet a few drawbacks of ships currently on the seas."

She nodded to herself. "I would very much like for you to draw up a list of things you would include in the building of a new ship, Captain Andrews. The whats and the whys behind them. Could you do so now? I am most interested to see your ideas and discuss them with James."

"I would be happy to do so, Your Grace."

The duchess rose. "Here. Use my desk." She began stacking papers, clearing a space for him to work. "You will find plenty of parchment in the top right drawer. How long do you think it will take you to compose your list?"

He thought a moment. "A couple of hours at most although I would reserve the right to add to the list in the future if anything came to me."

She glanced to the clock sitting upon the mantle. "It is nine o'clock now. I will return at noon for us to discuss this matter."

Drake got to work once she had vacated the room. First, he listed ideas that immediately came to mind. Then he closed his eyes, walking through *Vesta* from memory, starting at the gangplank leading up to the deck, going into every nook and cranny of the ship. As he did so, he jotted down ideas, excited that someone was interested in his opinion.

When she returned at noon, his list was complete. He had read over it several times, making a few changes, and then rewriting it in a neater hand, organizing it so that the list was prioritized.

Rising, Drake handed the duchess his notes. She sat behind the desk again.

"Let me read over this, then I will assume that I might have questions for you."

"Of course, Your Grace."

Not wanting to sit directly across from her as she perused it, he moved to the window, looking out at the gardens in the rear of the house. He thought of the time he had spent in these gardens with Dinah, in the gazebo, and a deep yearning filled him. He had yet to see her today.

And he could not imagine when the time came that he would not see her. For days. Months. Even a year or more.

His throat grew thick with unshed tears. He cursed inwardly, knowing he should never have gotten involved with her, and yet the past week had been the sweetest time of his life. No, he would not trade for the hours they had spent together. While he wished he could ask her to wait for him, seeing him between voyages, he thought it best when he left England this time to cut all ties with her. It was wrong to give her—and him—hope that they could have some kind of life together.

Lady Mirella's words echoed in his head, though. He knew the girl meant well, but she was not yet out in Polite Society. While she had good intentions, encouraging a relationship between him and Dinah, Lady Mirella had no experience with just how vicious gossip could be. Drake knew Dinah would never risk her girls' future merely for them to be together.

"Captain, I do have a few questions. Several, in fact," the duchess said. "I have made a few notes as I read your list. Might we go over them together?"

He returned to sit opposite her, and they spent two hours conversing about his ideas. Drake would explain the need for a change, and the duchess would play devil's advocate. She questioned him about everything, relentlessly, until he was exhausted.

Then she smiled. "You are very clever, Captain. Creative, as well. I think your ideas are simply brilliant."

"Which ones?" he asked.

"All of them," she said, smiling at him, the sternness gone from her voice. "I like how you possess knowledge no one else in my office holds. I also admire how you stood up to me. Too many times, those around me tell me what they think I wish to hear and not what I need to hear. You defended your ideas with passion. You spoke clearly and concisely. It makes my decision even easier than I supposed it would be."

Perplexed, he asked, "What decision might that be, Your Grace?" worried that his position as *Vesta's* captain might somehow be in danger.

"I want to offer you a new position, Captain Andrews. One which you are partially qualified for."

"I do not follow you, Your Grace."

"Simply put, I will need to replace Mr. Barnes. No one in my company had his experience, so I will have to search outside it to find his replacement. At the same time, you display a depth and breadth of knowledge that goes beyond what anyone in my shipping offices possesses."

She smiled at him. "I would like you to become my new Mr. Barnes, Captain. I will have much to teach you about certain sides of the business, but with the leadership you possess and your unique knowledge of ships and trade, I believe you are the right man to help me lead Neptune Shipping."

Stunned, Drake could only gape at her.

"I know you were not expecting such an offer. I did not know I would be extending it. I do realize you would have to give up your life at sea, but I believe you would live quite a rewarding one on land."

He shook his head in disbelief. This would be a way to continue to see Dinah, yet it would also mean giving up what he had worked his entire life to accomplish.

He met her gaze. "May I think upon it, Your Grace?"

"Certainly, Captain Andrews. This is a momentous decision on your part. Life-changing, in fact. For you, as well as my company. Once I bear His Grace's child, I know the time I can devote to my company will become limited. I need to have someone I can trust implicitly to help run Neptune Shipping efficiently. I will always be a part of the company and would still make all the major decisions, but as our family expands in the years to come, I will need to step back and devote more of my time to my husband and our children."

A thrill shot through him. An opportunity for something new. A chance to be with the woman he loved.

"I told Dinah that you had a unique perspective on things, issues which I had rarely—if ever—considered."

Immediately, he frowned. "You told her you wished to hire me in this capacity?"

She shrugged. "We talked about it briefly. I was impressed by our conversation at Shadowcrest and told her I might consider offering you some type of position in the shipping offices. That was before I received words of Mr. Barnes' heart attack. Now that he has passed, it is critical that I replace him with someone who not only has your perspective on matters, but I also believe you could quickly learn about the other end of the business under my tutelage."

Doubt filled him first, worried that the business part would be hard for him to catch on to. But then anger sprang within him. "Did Dinah ask you to find a place for me?"

"No, not at all," the duchess assured him. "Though we did speak about your feelings for one another. Frankly, I think this is a perfect solution. You could be together, instead of separated for months or years at a time."

His head swirled. Yes, he would enjoy the challenge of contributing his knowledge, while at the same time learning how to run a business. Drake would never have guessed this would have been a possibility, especially since he came from such humble beginnings. But as a seaman, he had trusted his gut over anything logical or rational over the years. It was this deep instinct within him that told him this woman offered him the position merely to keep him on land. And in Dinah's bed.

He could not deny that he was a proud man. While he felt perfectly capable of taking on such a role in the shipping company—and even would look forward to the challenge of doing something far from the familiar situation he had been in for years, he could not in good faith have this be the only reason such a position was being offered to him. It was wrong to leave the sea simply because of his feelings for Dinah.

"I'm afraid I cannot accept this offer of employment, Your Grace," Drake said stiffly, rising from his seat. "I have worked far too hard from the time I was a cabin boy, longing to helm my own ship someday."

Then he worried his words would cause her to dismiss him, and he would be without a ship at all. He couldn't go to James and ask to be made a captain of one of the vessels at Strong Shipping Lines. If he did so and James acquiesced, it would bring strife between his closest friend and James' wife.

"Will you keep me on as *Vesta's* captain?" he asked, trying to temper his tone.

She studied him a long moment. "If that is what you truly wish. But understand this, Captain. You have realized your long-ago dream. The goal you set for yourself to one day captain a ship came to pass. I am offering you a new opportunity, a role you could play in my company which could be both challenging and lucrative. It would also allow you to remain in London. With Dinah."

Knowing he might regret the decision for the rest of his life, Drake said, "While I thank you for the opportunity and your consideration, I would prefer to remain at sea, Your Grace. Will that be a problem?"

She eyed him sadly. "Only for you, I am afraid. You—and Dinah."

Ignoring her words, he asked, "When would you like *Vesta* to set sail again, Your Grace?"

Consulting the diary on her desk, she said, "You are due to leave the seventh of September."

Rising, Drake said, "If you have need of me before we sail, I will be staying on *Vesta*."

He bowed to his employer and escaped the room. His anger now ran deep, and he believed the two women had conspired to find a way to keep him in port. That the duchess was merely placating him, telling him she liked his ideas, when all along she realized he was nowhere near qualified to replace Mr. Barnes. He was not some puppet on a string, being maneuvered by the pair, and he would never dance to their tune.

Reaching the foyer, he started to the door when he heard Dinah call his name. He glanced up, seeing her at the top of the landing, love for him shining in her eyes.

Tamping down his regret, he curtly called out, "Good day, Your Grace," nodding to the footman, who opened the door.

Drake walked out that door—and out of her life.

CHAPTER TWELVE

DINAH FELT A part of her wither inside at the look she saw on Drake's face, not to mention the dismissive tone in his voice. She froze as she watched him leave the townhouse, and her gut told her it was very likely he had just left her life.

Now, she needed to learn the reason why.

She knew he had been with Sophie all morning and went to Sophie's office, not bothering to knock. Upon entering, she saw the grim look on her friend's face. The small grain of hope she had clung to instantly evaporated.

Moving to stand in front of the desk where Sophie sat, Dinah asked, "What happened with Drake?"

Tears welled in Sophie's eyes. "It is all my fault." She swallowed hard. "I offered Captain Andrews the position Mr. Barnes had held, wanting him to help me in running Neptune Shipping. Yes, he knows nothing about running a business, but neither did I when I wed Josiah. My husband taught me all I needed to know. With the Captain's life experience, though, I believe he could be a valuable asset to my company. He is intelligent. Bold. Decisive. With what I could teach him—coupled with his own personal knowledge—I think him the ideal replacement."

"But he turned you down," Dinah said dully.

"Not at first. He told me he wished to think about it, and I would have thought less of him if he did not want to ponder such a huge change in his circumstances."

Sophie met her gaze. "Then I made a terrible mistake, Dinah. I mentioned that I had spoken to you about this job offer."

Understanding dawned within her. "Drake is a proud man," she observed. "He believed you extended the offer because of me. Not because he was the right man for the position."

Sophie nodded wearily. "Yes, I am afraid so. Both he and James are cut from the same cloth. They are capable men who have stood on their own for their entire lives. Your captain thought I was asking him to take on the position not because I thought him qualified but because I did it as a favor to you. Or worse. That we had concocted this scheme between us."

She recalled when Sophie had offered Drake command of *Vesta*. How he had lacked in confidence, not certain he was up to the job. Dinah had encouraged him then and would have encouraged him now.

But it was too late. She had lost him. Forever.

"I am so sorry, Dinah," Sophie apologized. "A mere slip of my tongue—something which had not even factored into my decision—changed everything. I am hoping after a day or two, Captain Andrews will have time to ponder the situation further and even change his mind."

She shook her head sadly. "No, he will not do so. He is a very proud man. As it is, it would have been difficult for him to have given up his life at sea. It is all he knows. Besides, even if he were to take the opportunity you provided to him, it did not necessarily mean good things for the two of us."

When Sophie started to protest, Dinah held up a hand. "No, I told you that my priority must always be my girls. Even over my own happiness. A widowed duchess wedding a sea captain would be wholly inappropriate in the eyes of Polite Society. I have always lived for my girls, and I must continue to do so."

Dinah did not say just how empty her life would be without Drake in it, especially after the last of her girls did wed and leave the nest. She only wished they had had a proper goodbye. A final farewell kiss that she could remember for the rest of her life.

Going around the desk, she embraced Sophie. "Do not blame yourself for any of this. I won't let you." Dinah wiped away a falling tear. "But I reserve the right to cry on your shoulder every now and then for what I have lost."

Sophie took Dinah's hands in hers. "Just because you have lost your captain, it does not mean you still cannot find happiness with someone else."

Gazing steadily at her friend, Dinah asked, "Would you be happy with anyone other than James?"

Tears filled Sophie's eyes. "No," she whispered.

"Neither would I. At least I had a brief window of pure joy. I experienced what it was like to love and be loved. It gave me insight into what Pippa and Georgina now have with their husbands. More than anything, I am committed to seeing the rest of my girls make love matches."

Sophie looked at her helplessly. "How will you go on, Dinah?"

Resolve filled her. "As I always have. From the time I was ten and seven, I have gone it alone." She smiled wistfully. "But I will never truly be alone, because I have the girls, along with you and James."

She stepped away. "If you will excuse me now, I need some time to myself."

Dinah went to the gardens, sitting in the gazebo, surrounded by her memories of Drake.

>>>><<<<

DRAKE SHAVED AND then dressed for the day, his heart heavier than it ever had been. Misery poured through him, giving him an idea what the rest of his life would be like without Dinah in it. It had been two days since he had last seen her. Two days since he had ended what was between them.

Today, he would see her again at the funeral for Mr. Barnes. Dinah had once called Drake a coward when he attempted to walk away from her. She must think so little of him already, but he was determined to show up to this funeral and honor Mr. Barnes' memory.

Having had a couple of days to himself, he had done nothing but think. Part of him believed he had cut off his own nose to spite his face in turning down the Duchess of Seaton's offer to replace Mr. Barnes at Neptune Shipping. He still did not think he was the right man for the position. He also knew in his heart he was not the right man for Dinah, either. Theirs had been a brief interlude, two lonely souls coming together, despite their different stations in society, finding love. Drake would love Dinah Strong every day for the rest of his life.

Even he knew, however, that they were not meant to last. He should have kept his distance emotionally and merely taught her what she needed to know to go into her next marriage and find physical satisfaction. It had been a mistake on his part to become involved with her. To love her. He would suffer for that error the rest of his life.

He slipped into the coat of his captain's uniform and once again consulted the note the duchess had sent to him, informing Drake of the time and place of Mr. Barnes' funeral.

Leaving *Vesta*, he walked along the wharf and then turned north. After a few blocks, he found a hansom cab and took it to the church where the service would be held, seeing the Seaton ducal carriage standing in front of the house of worship. He arrived just as the service was starting and moved down the aisle, slipping into a pew about halfway from the front. He looked about, recognizing a few faces from the warehouse and shipping offices, but his gaze lingered on the front row. The Duke and Duchess of Seaton sat with a woman.

But there was no Dinah present.

He relaxed, thankful he would not have to see her. It made sense, her not attending. She had not truly known Mr. Barnes or anyone at Neptune Shipping. Drake wasn't surprised because, for the most part, women did not attend funerals often. The Duchess of Seaton's attendance merely spoke to the unusual kind of woman that she was, as well as to her close working relationship to Mr. Barnes.

Drake became lost in thought before realizing the service had concluded. He rose, as the others did, and began making his way down the aisle once more. The duchess had not written of any burial plans, and he supposed they would be private.

Pushing open the door, he exited the church, looking about for transportation back to the wharf. When he heard someone call his name, he turned, seeing it was Neptune Shipping's warehouse manager. They engaged in a brief conversation.

By the time it ended, Drake saw the Duke and Duchess of Seaton had emerged from the church, James escorting his wife and the deceased's sister. The duchess did not glance in his direction, but James most certainly did. He could see the disappointment written across his friend's face. He realized in turning down the position at Neptune Shipping, it had set into motion a series of events. Not only had his warm relationship with his employer changed, but James would take the side of his wife over his oldest friend.

Drake couldn't blame James. It was only natural. Dinah was a part of the Strong family, the one which James now headed. Someone James saw on a regular basis, along with his sisters and cousins. It had not struck him before that in pushing Dinah away, he would also lose James in the process. He decided he would complete his upcoming voyage on *Vesta*, but once he returned to England, he would seek employment elsewhere.

The only problem was that Neptune Shipping and Strong Shipping Lines were the largest employers in the industry in Great Britain. Then again, because he had worked for such a large line for so many years, it might prove easier for him to find another ship with a different company.

His gaze met that of his friend's, and Drake nodded brusquely, turning away and striding down the street. He decided to walk back to his ship. Though it was a long way, it would take up time in his empty day.

Once he arrived back at the docks, he stepped into The Falconer, a popular tavern. It was in this very tavern that he and James had been drinking when his friend began to learn of his origins.

Drake decided to lose himself in drink—and a woman.

He entered The Falconer, which was only partially full at this time of the afternoon. Business would pick up as day turned into evening. He couldn't remember the last meal he had eaten, so he ordered a bowl of stew, along with a loaf of bread and a large tankard of ale.

A comely woman brought him his food and drink, lingering, flirting with him. He let her know he would be available once he finished off his meal and attacked it with false gusto. Drake only managed to get down half of the greasy stew, and it set hard in his belly. He ate a few bites of the bread and drained the tankard, calling for another one, and then a third.

By now, the ale had loosened him up, and he winked at the barmaid. She returned to his table, telling him to meet her in the alley next to the tavern.

He gave her a coin, one that covered both his meal and the tupping they would do, and left. Standing in the alley, memories flooded him of all the times he and Dinah had been creative, making love anywhere but a bed. The thought of pressing a stranger against this wall and pounding into her caused a wave of nausea to strike him. Drake vomited the meal and ale he had just consumed and fled back to his ship.

When he reached it, he hurried up the gangplank, nodding at the sailor on watch. A handful of men rotated to guard *Vesta* when she was in port.

Making his way to his quarters, he opened the door. Much to his surprise, James Strong sat in the chair that had once been his.

"What the bloody hell are you doing in *my* chair?" he demanded.

James rose. "Forgive me, Captain Andrews, for taking your seat." His friend moved to sit in the only remaining chair in the cabin.

"I didn't ask you here, much less to sit," Drake said stubbornly.

"Well, you should have," James roared back, startling Drake. "I always knew you were thick-headed, Drake Andrews, but you have outdone yourself in foolishness and stupidity."

He reined in his temper, thinking this would most likely be the final conversation he had with the man he considered to be his brother.

"I am sorry you feel that way, Your Grace," he said formally. "You are living your own life now. You are no longer involved in nor responsible for mine."

"Do you know how bloody miserable Dinah has been the past two days?" James asked. "Of course, she thinks she is hiding it, putting on a brave face, but I know you broke her heart, Drake."

Anger surged through him. "Well, she broke mine, too," he shouted, tears stinging his eyes.

"Why did you turn down Sophie's offer?" James asked quietly.

His pride prickled at the question. "I am not qualified in any imaginable way to help your wife run Neptune Shipping, and you know it."

"You thought the same about being a ship's captain, and yet look how successful you have become," James pointed out. His friend paused. "You know how much you mean to me, Drake. How much I believe in you. I think you can do anything. Sophie does, as well. She has told me of the conversations the two of you have had. You would bring more to the position Mr. Barnes held than he ever could. Yes, Sophie knows you are raw and inexperienced as far as the business side of things go, but she is willing to teach you, just as Josiah Grant taught her."

James glared at Drake. "I want whatever is best for my wife—and that means if she wants you to help her run Neptune Shipping, then she will have it."

He laughed harshly. "Just because you're a duke now, you cannot force me to give up *Vesta*. Besides, even if I took Mr. Barnes' place and learned all your duchess could teach me, it still would not mean I could be with Dinah."

"Why?" James asked, shaking his head. "You are perfect for one another."

Drake collapsed on his bunk, worn out physically and emotionally. "She is a duchess. A bloody duchess, James. I am so far beneath her. Besides, more than she loves me, she loves those girls. She would die for them. She has seen her twins wed for love, and she wants that for the rest of them. But there wouldn't be a man in her world—your world now—that would even consider a marriage with one of them if Dinah were tied to me."

James opened his mouth to speak and closed it, seeming to finally understand the dilemma Drake and Dinah had found themselves in.

"So you see, it is impossible for us to be together. For me to make Dinah my wife," he continued. "This way, if I go out to sea and am gone for a year or two, she can move forward with her life. Even find a man to wed, one the *ton* would give their blessing to."

"No," his friend said. "*You* are the one who doesn't understand. I am a duke, Drake. A *duke*! You cannot begin to comprehend the power I now wield. There are but a handful of dukes in England, and we hold sway over others. I am only beginning to discover just what a force I am, now that I bear the title of Duke of Seaton. How by a few words, I can compel others."

James smiled at him. "I would never use this power for evil or personal gain. But will it override anything Polite Society has to say?

Absolutely. Would there be gossip with Dinah wedding you? Of course. Gossip is the lifeblood of the *ton*, but it would not keep you from accompanying Dinah to social events, nor would it hurt my sisters or cousins."

"How, James?" he demanded. "How could such a mismatched marriage not cause a scandal?"

"Because I am a duke," James said simply. "Because Dinah's girls are sisters and cousins to a duke. *Everyone* wants to be connected to a duke, Drake. Everyone. It doesn't hurt that the girls all have healthy dowries, as well as their blood relationship to me. And I can tell you now, those four will be awfully choosy when it comes to marriage, especially after having seen how happy Pippa and Georgie are in the matches they have made for themselves. They will not settle for anything less than love, just as I did.

"Just as you should do."

Drake felt the wind go out of him. Could it be true? Could James, by merely being a duke, simply trample over any gossip? He had no idea of the inner workings of the world his friend now lived in, but he doubted James would say these things unless they were true. Yet Dinah had always been part of Polite Society, and she had thought their relationship would cause trouble.

"Dinah seemed to believe if our relationship became known, it would damage her girls' chances of making a suitable match."

"Dinah was wed to my father. He was not a loving man by any means, Drake. I am certain he never showed her the true power he wielded. He might not have understood it himself." James' eyes gleamed. "But I do. I have also come to understand that family is everything. I love my sisters and cousins. I will make certain they have every opportunity to make the matches they desire. I have already made a few friends amongst the *ton*, Drake. Friends who will stand with me and support your union to Dinah, simply because I ask them to do so. Friends who would squash any gossip they heard about the two of you."

Hope sprang within Drake. Would it be possible to have everything he desired? Dinah as his wife. Being a stepfather to her girls. And changing the direction of his working life, from that of a sea captain to a man of business. Ever since Sophie had dangled the opportunity of a new career before him, Drake realized he had aspirations beyond his life now, ambitions he had never known lay dormant within him. If the possibility to remake himself professionally were possible, he might be a more presentable husband to Dinah. Need for her burned within him, not merely of a sexual nature, but the need to make her his constant companion. To be friend and lover and husband to the woman he loved would be life altering.

"What might you ask these friends of yours to do?" he asked, having not a clue as to how James might vanquish any gossip if Drake did wed Dinah.

"There is something known as the cut direct in Polite Society. If an influential member of the *ton* gives an individual the cut direct, then that person is ostracized. They are no longer invited to any social affairs. Their entire family is lumped with them. They are, in effect, banished to the country, never to be heard from again. If anyone deems to go against me—and your marriage to Dinah—then I have only to threaten to do this, and all gossip will die. *No* one seeks to alienate a duke, Drake." James smiled. "You should be glad such a powerful man calls you his brother. You are—and always will be—family to me. I would die for you."

A warmth spread through him, his dreams now within reach. "I would do the same for you, James. And I believe you. I believe I can have what I thought to be impossible, thanks to you."

His friend engulfed him in a bear hug. "Then we should go home to those we love, Drake."

He pulled away. "Do you think Dinah will still have me?"

"Why don't we go and find out?"

CHAPTER THIRTEEN

D INAH HAD TRIED to play the pianoforte and lose herself in the music, something Georgina and Mirella did with ease. She, however, was not the talent her two daughters were. Because of that, she failed in her mission to cease thinking about Drake Andrews. Everywhere she looked, something would remind her of the handsome sea captain that held her heart. She had eaten little and slept even less since she had last seen him.

"This has to stop," she told herself, determination filling her.

The Season was still in full swing. While she had made known she was out of town, which had prevented anyone from calling upon her, she would remedy that situation by attending tonight's ball. Ironically, it was being hosted by Lord and Lady Cowper. She wondered what the countess had shared about seeing her with Drake at Gunter's and decided it didn't matter. A month of the Season still remained, and Dinah would throw herself into the social swirl once again. While the house party she planned would honor Allegra and Lyric, it wouldn't hurt to invite a few gentlemen closer to her age. Perhaps they might help her to forget Drake.

She snorted at that thought. Nothing would ever cause her to forget the most magical week of her life.

Rising from the pianoforte, she decided to go to her room and allow her lady's maid to try out a few new hairstyles. Perhaps that would pull her from the rut she languished in.

As she crossed the room, the door flew open, causing her to halt in her tracks.

Drake . . .

Instantly, her heart pounded wildly. Worse, her core tightened, throbbing in anticipation of the intimate touches it knew because of him.

She clasped her hands, tightening them, trying to keep her wits about her, as she calmly asked, "Whatever are you doing here, Captain Andrews? If you have business to discuss, I am sure you can find Her Grace in her office."

He moved toward her in a slow, deliberate fashion. "My business is with you, Duchess," he said, his voice hoarse.

She wanted to flee. To avoid seeing and speaking with him. But her body betrayed her, and she remained rooted to the spot.

"We have no business," she said firmly, in a voice she used when her girls had been in a rare bit of trouble, her tone brokering no nonsense.

Drake reached her. His hands framed her face. Her body leaped at his touch, her breath jagged.

"I have been the greatest of fools, Dinah," he said. "I threw away two opportunities. One, to allow Her Grace to teach me all I would need to know in order to help her run Neptune Shipping. The other?"

His thumbs caressed her cheeks, and Dinah closed her eyes, relishing his touch. His warmth.

"I lost the chance to be with you. Truly be with you. Even married to you."

Instantly, her eyes opened as she sucked in a quick breath. Dinah stumbled back, not strong enough to hear him say such words to her.

For his part, Drake took a few steps forward, his hands taking her by the waist.

"You believed in me when I did not believe in myself, Dinah," he told her. "When Her Grace wished to make me captain of *Vesta*, I took strength—even comfort—from your belief in me. And you were right. I did have it within me to meet any challenges tossed my way. I am a good captain, Dinah. I know I could be a leader at Neptune Shipping."

He jerked her to him, their bodies colliding, stealing her breath.

"James convinced me that because of his ducal title, he holds sway over the people in your world. He told me about something he referred to as the cut direct."

Dinah gasped. The cut direct was always done publicly, effectively humiliating a person, ostracizing them and everyone in their family from Polite Society.

Drake smiled. "I see you know what I speak of. James loves his family, and that includes you. He would do anything for you and your girls, even use his influence to cast out anyone who dared to cross him. Or who gossiped about his family. As a duke, he said he can influence others and that he has made some powerful friends, as well. He promised me the girls would make excellent matches—love matches. That it would not matter if you and I wed because we would all fall under his protection."

Instinctively, she knew James would harness the power he had, even bring Polite Society to its knees, all to help her and her girls.

And allow her to find happiness with Drake . . .

"Can he do this, Dinah? Does James' title give him the influence he claims he possesses?"

"Yes," she said, her voice a whisper.

"Since James pledges to stand with us and see that your girls find lasting happiness, would you consider a future with me?"

Tears cascaded down her cheeks. "Yes," she said, her voice breaking.

"Will you marry me, Dinah? Will you put aside the hurt I have caused you and make me the happiest man alive?"

Through her tears, she smiled up at him. "Yes." She bit her lip. "I can hardly believe this is happening. It seems as if I am in a dream."

Drake smiled. "I have been merely existing since we parted, my life a living nightmare. Thank you for your forgiveness. I vow never to hurt you again, love. I will care for you. Cherish you. Love you. All the days of our lives. You and all the girls."

She threw her arms about his neck, bringing his mouth to hers. The kiss told her of the good man that he was and how he would always treasure her.

He broke it. "James told me of something called a special license. He said it would allow us to wed quickly, without waiting for the banns to be read."

"We can wait," she told him, knowing how expensive they could be and aware that she would have to consider that she wed a working man, albeit one who would help Sophie run a vast shipping empire.

"No, we can't," he told her. "Besides, James said it would be his gift to me, the brother of his heart. He has already sent word to Shadowcrest for everyone to come here for our wedding. He did not think you would wish to hold the ceremony there since your first marriage had taken place in its chapel."

She toyed with his hair. "You were that certain I would agree to wed you?"

"You had no choice, my dearest love. We were meant to write our love story for the ages."

Drake kissed her again, and Dinah knew from now on, all would be right.

⟫⟫⟩⟨⟪⟪

DINAH WATCHED AS James gave the gold wedding band to the clergyman performing the ceremony. He accepted it, resting it a moment on the Bible he held, and then handed it to Drake.

Her groom took her left hand and slid the ring onto Dinah's finger.

"With this ring I thee wed, with my body I thee worship, and with all my worldly goods I thee endow: in the Name of the Father, and of the Son, and of the Holy Ghost. Amen."

Another prayer began and as she closed her eyes, Dinah was grateful they wed in town and not in the chapel at Shadowcrest. She was no longer a Strong. She was now an Andrews, delighting in her new name.

The prayer concluded, and the clergyman told the assembled guests that the couple was now officially wed.

Drake bent, kissing her softly, his familiar lips against hers, giving her strength and bringing her a world of happiness.

She heard the applause around them and gazed about. Aunt Matty and Caleb had brought Mirella, Effie, Lyric, and Allegra up from Kent yesterday. Her girls had spent a few hours in Dinah's bedchamber last night, plying her with questions, assuring her how excited they were for her, telling her how radiant she was and how much they liked her choice of husband.

Dinah only wished Georgina and Pippa could have been here. Her marriage would be a surprise to both of them, but once they met Drake and saw how happy she was, she knew they would support her decision. She would write to both of them from Crestridge. After today's wedding breakfast, she and Drake were journeying to her small estate. He had been surprised she had her own country estate and was eager to see it.

Her new husband escorted her to the dining room, where Cook and Mrs. Powell had set up a buffet. Mirella told her she was composing a song as a wedding present, while Effie told Drake that teaching him to ride would be her present.

"Mama enjoys riding, so you will, too," her youngest daughter declared, causing everyone to laugh.

As they ate, Aunt Matty asked, "How long will you be in the country?"

"We will take a week at Crestridge," she said. "Then we will return to Shadowcrest. Sophie is composing a lengthy document of the most vital things Drake needs to know."

"Once we go over this document together, we will return to town," Drake added. "Dinah will stay a couple of weeks, and then she will go down to Shadowcrest to see to the house party."

"You will stay in town?" Allegra asked.

"For the first week of the party. I need to jump in, headfirst, and see to the running of Neptune Shipping since Sophie and James will be returning to the country today."

Dinah was grateful that Drake was finally using Sophie's given name. He had told the girls to call him Drake, but they seemed partial to calling him Captain, which he took in stride.

"After a week, my husband will travel to Shadowcrest and meet with Sophie regarding business. He will stay for the remainder of the house party, and then the two of us will return to town."

She had talked things over with the girls, explaining how most of her time would be spent in the city since that is where Drake's work was. James had persuaded them to take a set of rooms in the east wing, and so they would be living in the ducal townhouse a good portion of the year, visiting Shadowcrest and Crestridge whenever possible. Mirella and the twins were excited by the prospect of being in town more, while Effie said she would be perfectly content remaining at Shadowcrest for the most part. Dinah knew how much her youngest daughter loved the estate and her assortment of animals there. James and Sophie had agreed to keep an eye on Effie, as had Aunt Matty.

The wedding breakfast concluded, and Dinah said her goodbyes to everyone.

"Remember, I shall be at Shadowcrest soon," she reminded the twins. "I am already composing the guest list for your house party and will issue those invitations shortly."

She hugged and kissed everyone goodbye, with Mirella slipping her arm through Dinah's, walking her to the waiting carriage.

"Take care, Mama," she said. "Of yourself and the captain." Her daughter grinned. "We like him so very much. He is simply perfect for you."

"Thank you for saying so, Mirella," Drake said, joining them.

Mirella grinned at them. "I hope the two of you will give us at least another sister. Or perhaps a brother. James could use some male company in the family."

Dinah blushed at the thought, kissing Mirella goodbye and getting into the carriage.

Drake joined her and immediately asked, "Are you willing to have another child, love?"

"To be honest, I had not even thought of it. I am just so happy to have you. But surely, you might like to have one? I am not sure I can, Drake. I am three years shy of forty and would be two years shy when I gave birth. And that is if I conceived right away."

"You are in good health, but I will leave the decision to you, love."

She looked at him, seeing the love he held for her in his eyes. "I would like us to try for one. I hope that might be enough for you."

"It will be plenty. And if for some reason we aren't blessed in that fashion, I already have so many wonderful girls. Your girls are my girls, Dinah. I already love them as my own and can't wait to meet your twins."

He pulled her onto his lap, and she straddled him. "Hmm. This position looks familiar," she teased. "And we have yet to make love in a carriage, Husband. What do you say? Shall we try and make a babe on our way to Crestridge?"

Drake laughed heartily. "You are always full of good ideas."

Her husband kissed her, and Dinah knew there would be plenty of kisses—and plenty of love—in the years to come.

EPILOGUE

London—September 1811

D INAH ANDREWS FELT her water break, splashing down on the floor of the conservatory, something she had not experienced in over seventeen years. She had been so young then, wed to a duke who grew angrier each time she produced another daughter instead of the expected sons. Her hands went to her belly, protective of the child she carried within her, knowing her second husband, the love of her life, would lavish their child with both attention and love.

She took a deep breath, inhaling the sweet smells of the blooms surrounding her, already knowing what lay ahead since she had birthed four daughters.

She and Drake had decided they would try for only one child, due to her age. They had now been wed a little over a year, and she couldn't help but think it had been the happiest year of her life. Not only had both Lyric and Allegra found husbands whom they loved, but Mirella had, as well. Only Effie was left now, and Dinah wondered if her youngest, headstrong daughter would make her come-out next spring and take a husband. Effie had strong opinions. It would take a most unusual man in order for Effie to find happiness. And love.

Dinah left the conservatory, moving through the townhouse, returning to the set of rooms she and Drake shared. They had enjoyed living in James' London residence for most of the past year. Her husband's work at Neptune Shipping had kept them in town a majority of the time, with brief respites at Shadowcrest and Crestridge. Drake had thrived in his new role, managing Neptune Shipping under Sophie's guiding hand. Sophie herself had given birth to George, and as Drake proved most efficient, the Duchess of Seaton was handing over more and more of the business decisions to the former sea captain.

Dinah rang for Mrs. Powell and when the housekeeper arrived, she said, "You need to send for the midwife. It is time."

The older women smiled. "I will do so at once, Mrs. Andrews."

She could have continued being addressed as Your Grace by the staff, but Dinah wanted nothing to do with the title she had never sought, one which reminded her of her first husband. Seaton was dead, but he had gifted her with four lovely daughters. She stroked her belly, wondering if she would have another girl or if she would finally give birth to a boy. Drake had said he would be happy with either, and she knew he meant it.

Ringing for her lady's maid, she had the servant put her in a night rail. She slipped into a dressing gown, as well, the pains starting to come more regularly. Dinah had learned from experience not to lie abed too soon. That movement helped her in the birthing process, and even though she had not delivered a child in many years, she believed this one would come quickly since she had given birth before.

The midwife arrived, agreeing with her client that she should walk about a few minutes longer after hearing how far apart the pains were. As another labor pain struck her, though, Dinah clasped her belly, falling to her knees.

Suddenly, she was lifted in strong arms and carried to the bed. *Drake was here.*

"You should be at Neptune Shipping," she chided gently, not wanting him to see the agony that she could no longer hide.

He brushed her hair back. "Mrs. Powell sent for me. I had told her to do so when your time came. I plan to be with you every step of the way, love."

She smiled at him, a smile which turned into a grimace as another pain racked her body.

The midwife said, "We should remove your dressing gown, Mrs. Andrews." She looked pointedly at Drake. "And remove Mr. Andrews, as well."

As her husband lifted her from the bed and untied the belt on her dressing gown, pushing it from her shoulders and handing it to her maid, he said, "I was here when we made this babe together, and I will remain here as we see it come into the world."

The look he gave the midwife brooked no questions, and the woman nodded curtly.

"It is highly unusual for a man to remain in the birthing chamber," she told them, "but if Mrs. Andrews wishes it, so be it."

"I do," she said as pain gripped her again and the urge to push overwhelmed her. She looked to the midwife. "It is time for me to push."

"Very well."

Drake caressed her cheek tenderly and asked, "Where do you want me?"

Dinah thought a moment. "Behind me," not wanting him to witness the babe emerge from her body.

Instead of taking a seat in a chair by the bed or even perching on the bed itself, Drake removed the pillows behind her and climbed into bed with her. His legs went alongside hers, and he leaned her so that her back rested against his chest. His fingers laced through hers as Dinah brought her feet up, parting her knees. With the next pain, she pushed hard, groaning loudly as her hands gripped her husband's.

"Good, Mrs. Andrews," the midwife praised. "The head is crowning. I see a lot of dark hair."

With the next labor pain, she bore down even harder, pushing with all her might.

Drake's cheek rested against her temple as he said, "You are doing it, love. You are bringing life into the world again."

The midwife nodded, saying, "I see the shoulders. The babe is to the waist now. One more hard push, Mrs. Andrews, and your child will be born."

Exhaustion filled her, but determination won out. With the next pain rocking her body, Dinah grunted loudly, bearing down so hard that she felt the babe leave her womb in a quick rush.

Though weary, longing to close her eyes and rest, she watched as the midwife cut the cord and turned the babe upside down, lightly tapping its buttocks.

Immediately, a loud cry erupted from the newborn, causing her to relax even as her husband tensed.

The midwife turned away with the babe, washing it as Drake pressed his lips to her temple.

"You have done it, Dinah. You have given birth to our child." He chuckled. "Our very loud child."

She smiled, weariness filling her, still anxious to hold the infant as she felt the need to push again, expelling the afterbirth.

The midwife returned, the babe now swaddled. The woman placed the bundle into Dinah's arms, saying, "You have a healthy son, Mr. and Mrs. Andrews. Congratulations."

"A boy," she sighed, tears of happiness stinging her eyes as she glanced up at Drake.

He beamed at her and then turned his gaze upon their son. "A boy," he echoed. "A fine, fine boy. With a head full of dark hair."

She looked down at her son. Their son. Love swelled within her.

"We never talked about names," she said. "Do you have one in mind?"

Drake bent and brushed his lips upon the babe's brow. "I think we should name him James. For the man who has meant so much to the both of us. The one who convinced me that we belonged together."

Dinah thought of how, not only had they both held friendship with James dear to them—James had championed them and their marriage. Only one gossip of Polite Society had dared to speak ill of them, and James had personally given the woman the cut direct. She had become a social outcast, and not another soul had crossed the powerful Duke of Seaton. The rest of the *ton* had quickly fallen into step and welcomed Dinah and Drake with open arms.

"James," she repeated, looking at their babe with love. "Yes, I believe that would be a wonderful way to honor our friend. I have always liked the name myself."

"But we don't want him confused with his namesake. How about within the family, we call him Jamie?"

Dinah smiled as the babe opened his eyes, looking at them in curiosity as he began to coo.

"Jamie. I quite like it. What do you think of your mama and papa, Jamie?" she asked.

Her husband stroked the infant's cheek with one finger and said, "He thinks he is the most fortunate babe in the world because his parents love him and one another."

Drake's palm went to her cheek, cradling it, turning her toward him as he kissed her lightly.

"I love you now in this moment more than I ever have," he said huskily.

"And I love our family and you."

Her husband kissed her again, and Dinah knew a wonderful life lay ahead for the three of them.

About the Author

Award-winning and internationally bestselling author Alexa Aston's historical romances use history as a backdrop to place her characters in extraordinary circumstances, where their intense desire for one another grows into the treasured gift of love.

She is the author of Regency and Medieval romance, including: Dukes of Distinction; Soldiers & Soulmates; The St. Clairs; The King's Cousins; and The Knights of Honor.

A native Texan, Alexa lives with her husband in a Dallas suburb, where she eats her fair share of dark chocolate and plots out stories while she walks every morning. She enjoys a good Netflix binge; travel; seafood; and can't get enough of *Survivor* or *The Crown*.

Printed in Great Britain
by Amazon

43704161R00079